Late Bloom Summer

by

Michael Robert Wolf

Finishing Line Press
Georgetown, Kentucky

Late Bloom Summer

Publisher: Leah Huete de Maines
Editor: Christen Kincaid
Guest Copy Editor: Mindy Salkind
Background Cabin Image: Pixabay
Cover Design: Lisa Hoop
Author Photo: Darren Collis

Order online: www.finishinglinepress.com
also available on amazon.com
Author inquiries and mail orders:
Finishing Line Press
PO Box 1626
Georgetown, Kentucky 40324
USA

Contents

Chapter One...1

Chapter Two...4

Chapter Three...14

Chapter Four...18

Chapter Five..26

Chapter Six..32

Chapter Seven...40

Chapter Eight..46

Chapter Nine...50

Chapter Ten..55

Chapter Eleven..60

Chapter Twelve...66

Chapter Thirteen...71

Chapter Fourteen..75

Chapter Fifteen...80

Chapter Sixteen...85

Chapter Seventeen...90

Chapter Eighteen...94

Chapter Nineteen..99

Chapter Twenty...106

Chapter Twenty-One...111

Chapter Twenty-Two...115

Chapter Twenty-Three...118

Chapter Twenty-Four...123

Chapter Twenty-Five..127

Chapter Twenty-Six..130

Chapter Twenty-Seven..134

Chapter Twenty-Eight...137

Chapter Twenty-Nine 140

Chapter Thirty 143

Chapter Thirty-One 145

Chapter Thirty-Two 150

Chapter Thirty-Three...153

Chapter Thirty-Four...157

Chapter Thirty-Five..160

Chapter Thirty-Six..163

Chapter Thirty-Seven...167

Chapter Thirty-Eight..169

Chapter Thirty-Nine 173

Chapter Forty..176

Chapter Forty-One...181

Chapter Forty-Two...185

Chapter Forty-Three 189

Chapter Forty-Four 192

Chapter Forty-Five...194

Chapter Forty-Six...199

To Barb Richards, a true friend and talented administrative secretary who has touched my life as well as others for many years.

Chapter One

It is a demonstrable fact that, when it comes to human beings, there is no such thing as a tender age. It doesn't exist, despite the description. There are, however, several fragile ages, breakable ages—even crushable ones. And arguably the most brittle among them is the thirteenth year of life.

And that was Scotty Malnick's age, thirteen years old—no, not presently, not this year, or last year, or the year before—but far back in the sharp ninety-degree angle year of 1964—the post presidential-cranial-exploding, then suddenly mop-top driven year of 1964. It was as if someone had thrown a Beatle wig on Kennedy to obscure the mortal wound. That was the year. And to be specific, that was the summer of Scotty Malnick's thirteenth birthday, the summer of 1964.

Scotty sat stiffly in the inside seat of the grey chartered bus, watching his parents' parked car recede into the civilized distance. He could still feel his mother's tight hug. As it faded, so did his agnostic father Stanley's all-too-frequent hot-tempered use of God's name, which he knew he wouldn't be subjected to for several weeks. But in their place, unexpected loneliness began to envelop him—a kind of pre-homesickness. Already? Within seconds, it completely overtook him, and he began to tear up. Embarrassed and ashamed, he faced the window, and so didn't even notice the red-haired freckled boy sitting next to him. Even seated, it was clear he was taller than Malnick.

The thick crosstalk of several excited camper introductions and re-connections competed with the rising and falling motor torque and shifting gears. Scotty continued to face the window in silence, aware that he couldn't sustain that position for long—that is, without appearing to be a misanthrope. But he was in no mood to be the first one to introduce himself. Even amidst the grinding gears and giddy laughs, silence reigned awkwardly. Finally, he heard a raised voice next to him

"I'm Gus…Gus Simmons. Second summer."

Scotty wondered inwardly about the name.

That doesn't sound like a Jewish name for a Jewish camp. Sounds more like the astronaut Gus Grissom, and it's for sure he isn't Jewish. No Jewish astronauts in the Mercury Seven.

The Space Program was one of Scotty's main extra-curricular interests. He turned his body away from the window and half toward Gus, whose name seemed to fit him perfectly—what with his boxy looking face and crew-cut red hair. It was too soon for boys' hair styles to catch up with John, Paul, George, and Ringo. Scotty's hair was a bit longer, but by no means long, and dark brown.

"And you?"

Scotty was hoping that his eyes had dried enough to give away nothing of his raw emotions.

"My first."

He was still angry with himself for letting his mother talk him into leaving his one-child bedroom privacy behind to live for six weeks with twenty-five or so boys and one or at most two bathrooms. He knew his father was the reason, and that made him even angrier at *both* parents.

As Scotty peered fleetingly at the boys around him, he could tell that they were on their way to being men, with some of them clearly growing the dark shadow of developing beards. That would mean they had body hair elsewhere. He felt like a baby-faced infant among them. And he knew that feeling would only increase while undressing for bed in the revealing bare-bulb glow of the bunk lights.

Before long the gears were shifting again, as the vehicle began a gentle ascent at the foot of the Pocono Mountains. As their destination grew closer with every upward mile, Malnick noticed a young girl in the seat in front of him. A partial look at her face between the tall seats stirred curiosity to see more of it. From his vantage point, she already reminded him of a combination of Hayley Mills and Mick Jagger--whose face, with full lips and big eyes, looked particularly girlish in the summer of 1964. Her hair, like Jagger's, was dirty blonde and slightly curled—and like Mills', with subtle bangs.

Scotty sat back in his seat and closed his eyes. After a short pause, the awkward silence between him and Gus was interrupted by a straight black-haired dark complected twenty-something woman that reminded him of a Jewish Joan Baez. She began strumming on her folk guitar, as she sang songs that had inhabited every amateur folk singer-guitarist's repertoire over the past year—songs like "Will the Circle Be Unbroken," which seemed more like a Christian hymn to him than a Jewish camp song. But then again, folk songs could be about anything, he supposed.

The bus stopped once so everyone could use the bathroom at a Howard Johnson's truck stop. Scotty was glad to find an open stall instead of a urinal. Once out of the bathroom, he watched as a few fellow travelers purchased candy bars. But he wasn't in the mood to eat anything—even candy. Then everyone got back on the bus, and it continued toward its destination.

Chapter Two

The paved road narrowed to two lanes and then continued for maybe another thirty minutes. The bus slowed, then stopped, and then turned left under a sign that said *Camp Chalutzim*, or "Pioneers" in Hebrew. To Scotty, whose father had hammered into his mind the horrors of the Holocaust for as long as he could remember, it might as well have said *Work Makes Free*, the words on the sign at the entrance to Auschwitz. Only an adult with a grasp of the complete difference would recognize it as the opposite.

The bus labored over the road and then lumbered on the grass as it approached several cabins on its left and right, finally halting between them. The folk-singing counselor stood up, a sign that everyone should get off the bus. Scotty waited for Gus to move out of his seat, and then followed the line out. Girls to the right and boys to the left. Even that benign act reminded him of his father's concentration camp accounts. Why did he let his parents persuade him to spend the summer at anything called a "camp"?

The bus driver performed double duty, pulling camp trunks out of the hold. As they were removed, everyone began examining tags to find theirs. So many looked alike. His was one of the last. Others' trunks, including Gus' and "Hayley Mills," were already being dragged up the few wooden cabin steps by the campers. He grabbed his by the leather handle and followed the others. It felt like a ball and chain. When he finally entered the cabin, he hesitated as he watched the boys choose beds that looked more like infirmary cots in a primitive hospital ward. The thin-as-pancake mattresses barely covered iron frames—with folded stiff-looking bleached white sheets, pillow covers, and olive-green "army barracks" blankets on one end—and flat-looking "prison-striped" pillows on the other.

There were three double-decker bunk beds in the room. They were already taken, which was fine with Scotty. He had no interest in either climbing up and down from the top or having someone else ascend to the top bed or descend from it—interrupting his sleep like a clumsy wingless angel. He diverted his eyes from the occupants of the double-decker beds and focused them on the boy who had taken the bed next to his. He realized that he might as well introduce himself, since their beds would be inches apart the whole summer.

"Um…I'm Scotty. Scotty Malnick."

The boy turned around and faced him. He had an almost cherubic face, with hazel eyes and dimples. His hair was brown and curly, and he had a Levitical nose—not large, but certainly Mediterranean. He gave the tiniest hint of a smile.

"Brandon. Brandon Marks."

Scotty repeated the name in order to remember it among the others. After all, they would be bunk mates.

"Brandon Marks."

Brandon clarified what he correctly supposed was a mental misspelling.

"Yes. *Marks.* M-A-R-K-S as opposed to M-A-R-X."

"Right. Um…"

He paused and then stated the obvious.

"Malnick. M-A-L-N-I-C-K."

"Of course."

"Right."

The conversation was over. The other boys had already started unpacking, and a few were making their beds. Scotty figured he'd better catch up. He opened the trunk and began taking clothes out. Seeing names sewn onto everything from shirts to shorts to underwear produced a strange sensation. What was it? He stared at a tag. Was this the only shred of his personal identity left in this room of strange boys? No. It wasn't that. He realized what it was—the invasive eyes that would see his most private apparel while they were being separated from everyone else's. That was it. These more mature boys would be that much closer to discovering his secret.

Dinner went better than expected. The concrete construction of the dining room—the *chadar ha-o-chel*, pronounced with the guttural ch—sonically reflected the campers' excited conversation, and produced a cacophonous wall of sound like a Phil Spector recording. Scotty thought it best not to compete with it. Back home, he wasn't known for being shy. But he didn't feel like talking in this cavernous echo chamber. After a quick one sentence Hebrew prayer, one he'd heard often in his synagogue, dinner was served. He realized only then that he was hungry. The flat thin kosher burger tucked into the puffy kosher bun tasted surprisingly good, especially with sweet-if-soggy corn on the cob. And the artificial grape drink was at least sweet. He ate in silence. He had only reached out to Gus, who was on the other end of a long table. So Scotty busied himself with his first Camp Chalutzim meal. After everyone was finished, a small booklet was passed out, and everyone started singing a kind of grace after meals—in Hebrew. Everyone except Scotty, that is, who'd never learned it and just stared down at the book, trying to follow along with a Hebrew word here and there. He would end up learning most of it by the summer's end. But he felt like an alien Gentile on this first night.

The rest of the evening was uneventful…until bedtime. However, he avoided embarrassment there by undressing and changing into his pajamas so fast that Superman could have taken lessons from him. As he lay in bed listening to choruses of crickets through the screened windows, he felt a slight cool breeze brush his face. That wasn't unexpected, considering their mountain location. The loneliness caught up with him. His eyes moistened again. He looked to his left and then his right, just making out the breathing, blanket-covered boys who seemed somehow to have already accommodated themselves to the dank outdoor summer air and the accompanying sounds of crickets.

Then he looked to his left again. He could just see a flashlight beam that bled through the cover of the boy next to him—the one whose name he'd memorized—Brandon Marks. Yes, that was his name. It was obvious that he was reading a book of some sort, or maybe a magazine. Perhaps it was something questionable, something Marks wouldn't want others to see, like a dirty novel, or a *Playboy* magazine. Or maybe the boy was just an avid bookworm, who liked to read before going to sleep. The secrecy aroused curiosity in Scotty. But those thoughts finally faded, and he fell asleep on this first night away from his cozy beloved bedroom.

Upon waking, the chill dawn air he usually associated with late fall involuntarily caused him to cover his face with the blanket—like a clam shutting its shell at the hint of danger. The temperature was, in fact, in the low forties—just ten degrees above thirty-two degrees Fahrenheit, the freezing temperature. He wanted to stay in bed the rest of the day, cocooned even when everyone around him finally shed their bed covers— which hadn't yet occurred. He listened to the arrhythmic sound of snoring which emanated from various points around him—until the obviously amplified sound of a composition he would never quite get used to even after a summer of it—reveille—blasted through the screened windows. Da da dit-dit dah, da da dit-dit dah, da da dit-dit dah, dit da da. He had hoped to quickly throw on a shirt, pants, and sweatshirt, and hit the bathroom before anyone else woke up. But his timing was off. Maybe tomorrow would work out better. Others were already getting dressed. A few resorted to their covers to change, preferring modesty. He was about to follow their lead when his covers were abruptly, if not violently, removed, leaving no room between his pajama-clad body and the icy air. He peered through his bleary eyes. The counselor, whom he had been introduced to with the rest of the boys, but hadn't yet said a word to, peered back at him. He was perhaps twenty-one, with a sun-freckled face, and medium length brown curly hair topped with a rainbow-colored knit yarmulke—a new sight for a boy who was only used to the black rayon ones distributed at his conservative synagogue. In one hand he carried a clipboard loaded with yellow lined legal paper, and in the other he held a pen.

"Okay. Judging from a process of elimination, you are either Jimmy Glazer or...."

He looked at the clipboard again.

"Scott Malnick."

The response was so soft, its bearer could hardly hear it.

"Malnick."

"Once again?"

"Malnick."

"Okay. I'm Shlomo. But you know that."

Somehow, Scotty didn't. But he didn't want everyone else, who apparently did, to know he didn't. Shlomo continued.

"Very good. Get dressed. Shacharit prayer is in fifteen minutes. You have your *tefillin*?"

Shlomo was referring to the leather boxes containing Hebrew words, worn on the forehead and right arm.

"I...I didn't know..."

Low but nevertheless piercing laughter resounded from all sides. Scotty knew what the boxes were, but he didn't know he was supposed to bring them to camp. Rarely ever touched, and right at this moment on his father's bedroom bureau, was a velvet bag containing the tefillin, the little boxes with leather straps, along with another velvet bag containing a *tallis*, or prayer shawl—just this very year of 1964 being pronounced tallit in America, following Israel's lead. His synagogue hadn't caught up yet, but Camp Chalutzim was ahead of the game.

Why hadn't his parents told him to bring them? They got him into this whole uncomfortable mess, and now they left him without necessary things everyone else had obviously brought in their trunk—items as second nature to them as their toothbrushes.

Shlomo spoke with closed eyes, which Scotty realized was better than rolling them.

"You had your bar mitzvah this last year, right?"

Scotty froze. Shlomo took that to mean yes.

"I hope you got a lot of presents…for nothing, apparently."

He took the continued silence to mean either Scotty had left the tefillin at home or had never received them. After unbearable silence, Scotty confirmed the former.

"Um…they're on my dresser."

Shlomo looked at the rudimentary chest of drawers by his bed that could barely be called a dresser.

"Are they the invisible type?"

"Um…I mean, they're on my dresser at home."

"They won't do any good there, now will they? We'll lend them to you for the summer."

"And your tallit?"

Scotty was relieved to answer that question in the affirmative.

"It's in my drawer…here at camp."

"Well, that's good to hear."

That ended *that* crisis. But it led to the next one, as Scotty followed everyone to the *Beit Tefillah*, literally the house of prayer. It was a short walk from the cabins. Scotty wished it was longer. Once inside the pine and cedar structure, Scotty saw familiar items—although smaller in dimension than he was used to. A rigged up *eternal light*, a small amber electric light in a clear glass-enclosed cage, hanging by a chain above what seemed to him to be a miniature Ark of the Covenant, or wooden box with open doors—and inside, a pint size Torah scroll, covered by the recognizable blue velvet cover. His camp mates took seats on smooth pine benches. One of the counselors, not his, handed out prayer books, or siddurim. Things got started very quickly. Scotty supposed everyone was hungry for breakfast. He knew he was.

The service got underway with some familiar prayers, particularly the well-known "Hear O Israel" chant from Deuteronomy 6. Soon after that, things went every which way—especially during the silent standing prayer, the *Amida*, which actually means *standing*. A number of the boys seemed to take it quite seriously, periodically rocking forward and back and side to side, and then bending their knees in something called *davening*—as he was later told—whenever they quickly mumbled God's name in Hebrew, or at least a Hebrew substitute for it. Scotty noticed, in particular, one of the more "serious" daveners, a slender boy with straight long brown side-locks wrapped over his ears. This tradition, an interpretation of the Torah command for men not to shave the corners of their beards, resulted in an odd combination of short hair on top and long hair over the ears.

Then Scotty's eye happened to catch Brandon Marks. He was rocking, but *just* rocking—not like the others. He seemed to be more scanning through the prayer book than chanting. And he nodded—not exactly like those around him, but more as if he was agreeing with this and that. And then he sat down before the others. That seemed strange to

Scotty, but he soon realized that anyone who finished just sat down. He did the same, shutting his eyes. It may have appeared to the observer that he was lost in prayer, but actually he was lost in thought.

"What have I gotten myself into?" was the first.

After prayer came breakfast. The loud cacophony was like dinner, but perhaps louder. The breakfast consisted of papery scrambled eggs that seemed fake. But the pancakes tasted real, which was good. The orange juice, however, seemed as fake as the eggs. But he was glad to be eating instead of dressing and undressing in the cold cabin. And the grey sweatshirt with the stylized Israeli flag-blue Chalutzim logo provided adequate insulation—*just* adequate.

After breakfast came about ten minutes of the same exact prayer that was sung at dinner. Scotty quickly realized that was the plan for every meal. The melody seemed catchy enough. And the bouncy repetition of the words *Kee L'Olam Chasdo,* for *His mercy endures forever,* lent a campy atmosphere to the proceedings—literally.

Then, after a half-hour of rest time to digest the meal, came baseball. Each boy got his mitt out from his belongings. Scotty's mitt seemed to lack the same maturity as his body. Everyone else's seemed muscular and well-worn compared to his small flat-looking glove. It seemed more like a plaything, a child's toy.

By the time Scotty—who was in the rear with Gus and Brandon—got to the field, Shlomo was standing at attention, clipboard in hand. He began a roll call.

"Berman."

"Hineni."

"Backman."

"Hineni."

Each boy spoke the same Hebrew word Abraham had used when God called him four thousand years ago. *Hineni.* "I'm here." Scotty took note. That way, he would save himself the embarrassment of not knowing how to respond in Hebrew when his name was called. Not being at the beginning of the alphabet had its definite benefits. At any rate, he knew the word hineni from Hebrew School. He waited for his turn in the alphabetical list.

"Hineni."

At any rate, that went well. After the roll call, Shlomo divided the group of 19 boys in half by telling them to count off in Hebrew, creating two teams.

"Achat."

"Shtayim."

"Achat."

"Shtayim."

Scotty was less nervous this time. But he knew that more embarrassment lay ahead…just ahead. Shlomo put on a Camp Chalutzim ball cap to shield himself from the rising summer sun. Almost all of the other boys had hats, and they put theirs on. Scotty had left his in the cabin. After all, it was still early in the day, and a gentle mountain breeze eased the slowly rising temperature and humidity. He *so* wished he hadn't left his hat behind, but it was too late.

Shlomo tossed a softball in the air a few times, snagging it with the net of his mitt like a shark snapping up a trout. Then he trotted several yards away from the group and began to call them one by one. As each boy was called, he walked a few yards from the others. Scotty suddenly realized that Shlomo was about to play catch with them, one at a time. *Oh no!* Once again, he felt like he was standing naked in the morning light…only in this case, the bright sunlight.

Shlomo chose to throw the ball instead of using the bat that was near him on the ground. Scotty waited for it to come his way, like a condemned man in front of a firing squad awaiting a piercing bullet. One by one, boys all around Scotty began snapping the ball up and firing it back in Shlomo's exact direction. Sometimes they adeptly fielded a grounder, and sometimes they caught a pop-up or fly ball. Then, suddenly, a line drive headed right for Scotty. It flew just by him, just inches from his head, like a guided missile. Gus ended up snagging it just feet behind Scotty and throwing it back to Shlomo, all in one smooth motion, like a robot in a science fiction movie. In fact, all of the others also seemed like robots, as if they were programmed to play pro ball. As it turned out, Brandon Marks fared no better than Scotty. He seemed equally as uncoordinated. At least there was one person who was as awkward as he was. That's the moment Scotty and Brandon became buddies.

Chapter Three

Scotty wasn't sure what came after baseball. Frankly, he didn't care. The immediate future lay in someone else's hands. Like a prisoner in a chain gang—without the chain—Scotty was condemned to serve out his summer sentence, traipsing from one involuntary task to another. He was sure everyone else knew what came next. He, however, didn't even *want* to know. But it wasn't long before he found out.

Somewhere between the baseball diamond and the *chadar ha-o-chel* stood a one-story wooden structure, a kind of little one room schoolhouse. Above the door, the Hebrew word *Keetah*, or classroom, was engraved with a burning tool on a wooden plank. Scotty, along with Brandon, Gus, and his other bunkmates, slowly single-filed into the room. Through one of the side windows, he could just catch a glimpse of "Hayley Mills'" soft Mick Jagger hair—full of sparkling highlights and Prell shampoo body. So, the class was co-educational. At least that would make things *somewhat* interesting.

The chairs were the kind with attached writing surfaces on the right side. They seemed out of place for a summer camp.

*So…*not only was he in a bunk surrounded by boys with body hair. He was also in a classroom surrounded by students who probably knew a lot more Hebrew than he did—and some of them were *girls*. He slid into one of the chairs behind and to the left of the subject of his growing interest.

A forty-something round-faced woman with graying Brillo Pad hair walked into the room and directly to the front, chalk in hand. Without saying a word, she began to hand out workbooks. He could see the words *Evreet Gimmel,* third level Hebrew, and under that the words *Modern Hebrew Conversational Workbook.* Scotty took the book and immediately flipped it open. He knew how to read Hebrew. Thankfully, there was no problem there. Unlike English, Hebrew keeps consistent phonetic rules. Anyone who learns the sounds of the letters can pronounce the words perfectly. At the same time, a student might also understand little to none of what they are reading or speaking.

Scotty was in the "little" category. Like a 1980's early Apple Lisa of many years later, he was programmed to haltingly speak what he saw written on the page—that, and the ability to recognize and respond to a few key commands like "Ma shlomcha?" ("How are you?") with the response "Kol b'seder" ("Everything is in order"). There were others in the summer class who seemed to be in his exact position, so at least he wouldn't be alone in his ignorance. However, he knew ignorance wouldn't be tolerated for long. He fully understood, having taken French One…two times… that he would be expected to memorize, every day during the week all summer long, Hebrew words taken from a list written out at the beginning of each chapter. He'd been in this position before. But that was during the school year. It didn't take long for Scotty to conclude that memorizing like this would devour the rest of his precious summer vacation. It was one of the things about Camp Chalutzim that he was quickly growing to despise, along with dressing and undressing, using the bathroom, and the ever-present loneliness.

Then again, there was Brandon. He seemed friendly, on the bus and since. And there was this girl, whatever her name was. He began to concentrate on her hair, which seemed to almost have a life of its own. Yet it needed the face it embellished to truly shine and shimmer. That face—the prettiest face he thought he had ever seen in a pre-teen girl—or *any* girl for that matter. He longed to connect a name to that face. But that would have to wait. Asking anyone was completely out of the question.

Scotty was awakened from his reverie by giggles behind him and on both sides. The teacher with the Brillo Pad hair, whom he had learned went by the name Geveret (Mrs.) Brombeck, was staring at him.

"Mr. Malnick. Mr. Scott Malnick. What are those two things on the sides of your head?"

"What?"

"Do you know what they are? Ears, Mr. Malnick. Ears. *Azna-im.* For listening."

The class laughed all at once, like a simultaneous staccato string section. It was painfully prolonged and only ended when Geveret Brombeck shouted above the *strings, "Shecket,"* which means quiet.

"We'll have no more of that. Where are your *derech eretz,* your manners?"

Then she turned back to Scotty.

"Mr. Malnick, from now on, I will ask you to concentrate instead of daydreaming. Please memorize the short list for our next class. That's all for today."

That was it? Class was over? Yes, that was it—for the first day. Everyone started to grab their primers and leave. Scotty couldn't wait to get out of there, no matter where the next "there" was. But overwhelming shackles of shame held him down. He felt like a bloodied boxer. Then suddenly, and unexpectedly, *the* girl, who also remained inexplicably seated, turned around.

"It's okay, Mr. Malnick. It's okay. I'm Sandy. Sandy Singer. I know how it feels."

Sandy. So *that* was it. The perfect name for her light, breezy-cream complexion and brilliant blue eyes—like a pristine shoreline on a sunny summer day. And Singer fit perfectly. It was the name of a celebrity. And Scotty was her biggest fan. Sandra would work too. Sandra Singer. It was a better name by far than the comparatively weak Sandra Dee. His face reddened as he drank in the nectar of her kindness. He shut his eyes. He could feel tears forming. This was the *worst* time for that to be happening! He couldn't very well wipe them without calling attention to himself. They streamed from his closed eyes and down his cheeks.

"Here's a tissue. I've got to go, and so do you."

She pulled a tissue out, as if by sleight-of-hand, and gave it to him. Then she was gone. He lifted his hand to his face and wiped the tears. Then he savored the next minute or so. Right there in Camp Chalutzim, he was experiencing feelings he'd never experienced before.

Chapter Four

Scotty's favorite time of day at Camp Chalutzim was the hour after lunch called free time, *Z'man Chofshee*. Just the name alone, in English or Hebrew, evoked emotions similar to those the Hebrew slaves must have felt as they took the first steps beyond the standing walls of the parted Red Sea. The camp observed a Saturday Shabbat, but that didn't seem to him like a time of rest. Just like the weekdays, he had to be on his guard. *This* time was his only true Shabbat—this short hour or so every day after lunch.

During the third day of *Z'man Chofshee*, Scotty discovered his own *Fortress of Solitude,* where he, like Superman, could find a little respite from his summer of suffering. In his longing to find his own space, he came upon a small path near the camp's entrance that navigated through a patch of tall grass. It was the perfect place to be left alone.

As he stood in the secret path, hidden like vulnerable prey from surrounding predators, he entered a mental land of make-believe worthy of Mr. Rogers' Neighborhood of some years later. He pulled up a plantain weed and looped the stem around itself, "firing" the head a few feet like a benign gun—decapitating it in the process. He imagined that his act was being whisper-narrated by a sports commentator.

Mr. Malnick is the present world champion. One look at his technique, and the reason becomes obvious. It takes literally years to develop. Okay. He's just about ready now. He's looping the stem with a style all his own. He's pulling the stem back in the loop. He's about ready and…fire! Nice form. The monitors are checking, and…yes! Scott Malnick has just broken the plantain weed stem distance world record! The fans are going wild!

Scotty's hour of personal sports ended with mild dread. It was time to go back to the cabin, only to await the next opportunity for possible embarrassment. What would it be? He tried to be as stoic about it as a thirteen-year-old boy could be. What difference would it make? Was there any way to numb his raw emotions so he no longer cared about anything or anyone, even himself?

As he trudged through a field and arrived at a dirt path leading to the cabins, his dark thoughts were joined by darkening clouds, as large drops of rain began to descend from a quickly darkening sky. What started as a rhythmic pattern quickly evolved into a driving summer deluge. Such pop-up showers are not uncommon in the Pocono Mountains. And their lengths vary. This one didn't give any indication of slowing down. Scotty's clothes were sponging up the soaking downpour. Running was useless.

By the time Scotty got to the cabin, he was drenched. He wasn't the only one who found shelter from the storm in the cabin. Some of the boys had arrived before him and were stripping naked in broad daylight. He couldn't very well climb between his sheets in this state. He had no choice but to expose his smooth hairless body to every prying eye in the room.

Suddenly, he got the brilliant idea to grab the large beach towel in his drawer and wrap himself with it. He was sure the act would draw more attention than if he paraded himself all over the room. But as it turned out, everyone else was busy changing, and no one else seemed to want to be accused of staring. He dispatched the business as quickly as he could. When that was done, and he had donned a dry tee shirt and jeans, he turned to see Brandon Marks—who had already changed into his dry clothes and had towel-dried his hair. He was kneading some sort of soft white ball in his hands. It certainly wasn't a soft or hardball. Scotty's curiosity was piqued.

"Hey…what's that?"

"Clay."

"No, it's not."

Brandon continued to knead as if he was in the process of baking a small loaf of bread.

"Well, it's my own invention…my own version of clay."

"Oh, come on. Where'd you get it?"

"I'll show you."

He put the newly formed ball on his dresser and reached next to it for his bottle of "no tears" baby shampoo and his container of baby powder.

"You see these?"

"Yeah, I see them."

"Well, I mix them together by taking some shampoo and putting it into a dixie cup. Then I add some powder and stir with a plastic spoon. After that I tear the cup and take the mixture with my hands and knead it like bread. The result…"

He produced the result.

"Clay."

"So, what do you do with it?"

"Nothing. I make balls and play with them…sort of. Someday soon I'll make a sculpture. I'm just practicing now."

"That's silly."

"No, it's not."

It was obvious to Scotty that his words had hurt Brandon. He could tell because Brandon's mouth quivered ever so subtly. Brandon turned away from him. Scotty knew he had to say something. Just above a whisper—in case anyone else was listening, he said, "I'm sorry."

Brandon looked at him and smiled.

"That's okay. It takes some getting used to. Maybe you should try it sometime. It makes a nice indoor activity on a rainy day…like today. My older sister showed me."

"Maybe I will."

Scotty searched for what to say next. After the awkward result of his painful words, he didn't feel comfortable either prolonging the conversation or cutting it short. Not knowing what to say, he just thought of the first thing that came to his mind.

"What are we supposed to do next?"

He figured Brandon would probably know the schedule. *He* certainly didn't.

"Israeli dancing."

"Israeli *what*?"

"Israeli dancing. It's not bad. You get to touch a girl, if you like that sort of thing."

"Dancing with a…*girl*?"

"Yeah. Maybe you'll get that Sandy girl. She's a knock-out."

Apparently, Brandon had also noticed her.

"Yeah. But I don't know how to dance that Israel stuff."

"I think they teach you."

"Oh."

All Scotty could think about was how dancing would provide another opportunity for embarrassment. Brandon laid down on his back and closed his eyes. Scotty thought he would end the conversation with a question.

"Um…I was just curious. What book was that I saw you reading under your covers last night?"

Brandon stiffened nervously and looked over at him.

"I'll tell you some other time."

So, it was a dirty book. Or was it? Brandon's response just made Scotty that much more curious. But he was so occupied with his own insecurity that he didn't ask anything further. He also didn't notice the sun, which had switched places with rainy clouds and was streaming through the open windows. The Orthodox boy, whose name turned out to be Benjamin Kahn, or Benny, looked through one of them and exclaimed loudly, "Look! A rainbow. A sign of HaShem's blessing!"

Scotty didn't know about that. But he was interested in seeing this natural phenomenon that he had only seen once or twice before—and *that* when he was much younger. He walked out into the now clear blue day and, sure enough, there was the wide rainbow arc. It almost touched the ground on one side and reached a grove of trees on the other. It did seem like a miracle of some sort, but not at all like a blessing. Nothing about this place seemed like a blessing—except maybe Sandy, the girl with the Hayley Mills hair.

The remnants of the summer shower had almost evaporated by the time the boys left the cabin for the asphalt basketball court, where the girls were waiting for them. The sun responsible for the evaporation was already creating perspiration that kept everyone's skin wet. The result was sticky hair like salty cotton candy, and saltwater-blinded eyes. With both girls and boys in that uncomfortable state, an hour or so of compulsory Israeli dancing commenced. A pop-and-hiss punctuated 33 1/3 RPM vinyl recording provided a lo-fi accompaniment. Geveret Brombeck was the mistress of ceremonies, speaking through a mic into the same distortion-emitting amplifier as the vocal/accordion mix.

"Okay, everyone. Shecket! Listen up. The song is called Erev Shel Shoshanim. Boys step, girls mirror. Walk, walk, step, rock, one quarter pivot to face partner. Like this."

Brombeck put needle to groove and then quickly stepped forward on the court as Shlomo joined her. Shlomo stood behind her and reached his hand up and over to join hers. As the music started, he turned around and faced her. Then, as a thin-voiced woman with an Israeli accent began to sing, they stepped with each other in sync with the recording. It seemed as if they liked each other. But Scotty couldn't tell for sure. They looked into each other's eyes whenever they faced each other. Scotty watched nervously.

They aren't gonna make me do that. No way.

He looked around him at the others. A few on each side of the sexual divide were nervously giggling. Sandy just stood, motionless, her eyes focused intently on Geveret Brombeck. She began to step lightly to the music, swaying elegantly as she danced. Suddenly, Geveret Brombeck stepped back from Shlomo and pulled the tone arm from the turntable with one swift motion.

"Alright. You and you, you and you, you and you."

She was pointing to boys and girls, one after the other. She directed them to one side, as Shlomo had the two baseball teams.

Are they gonna do this all summer, choosing sides for me? I just want to get out of here and go home. I hate this! I hate this whole camp thing! I hate it!

Scotty was preparing to walk away, intending to give the old bathroom excuse if he was noticed. Even if everyone rolled on the ground laughing, it would be worth it to get out of this even more embarrassing situation. As he prepared to leave, it suddenly occurred to him that Brombeck might choose Sandy for him. That elicited two responses. Number one, this was an opportunity to get close to the prettiest girl in Camp Chalutzim. Number two, it would result in a sweat-infused nightmare.

"You…and her."

Geveret Brombeck pointed to Gus and Sandy. That ended any possibility of Scotty dancing with Sandy, which was probably a good thing for him on such a hot day—and perhaps for Gus as well. Then, in rapid-fire succession, she pointed to one camper after another, directing them toward their chosen partner and arranging them in a circle with her at the center. She was the circus ringmaster with a whip, and they were the trained beasts. Scotty ended up with a squat moon-faced girl who it turned out went by the name Bunny.

"Bunny, Scott. You two! Come on! Bo Heyna. Quickly!"

Scotty hesitantly approached Bunny. They stood facing each other, their hands glued to their sides like robots in the off position. Geveret Brombeck walked over and positioned the two stiff automatons—or perhaps even more accurately, two mannequins from a discount department store, one from the chubby girls' section. Scotty's eyes were fixed just beyond Bunny's face, and he was sure Bunny's were similarly focused. Brombeck took Scotty's left hand and placed it in Bunny's right hand. It felt pudgy, like a baby's, and yet ice cold like an old maid's. Geveret Brombeck withdrew to the center of the circle. Scotty wondered how Bunny's hand could be so cold on such a warm day. Then Geveret Brombeck pulled Shlomo into the center.

"Watch our feet. Slowly-slowly to practice. One-two-three-four. Erev Shel Shoshanim. Ready…"

They exaggerated the steps like dramatic Japanese Kabuki dancers. After a few measures of pantomimed performance, Geveret Brombeck shouted loud enough to damage Shlomo's ears.

"Now, *you!* All of you!"

Scotty refused to move, causing Bunny to step squarely on his soft sneaker toe-cap. She breathed out an almost imperceptible apology.

"Sorry."

Scotty looked over at Gus and Sandy. They didn't exactly seem to be enjoying themselves. If they had been, Scotty wouldn't know what to do with his emotions.

The agony continued through two more Israeli folk tunes,

complete with step-by-step dance instructions—a kind of disoriented Arthur Murray class. During one step, Scotty came closer to Bunny than he ever had to a girl. For less than a second, his chest pressed against her bra, and the odd and awkward sensation caused him to instinctively pull back. He was sure his embarrassment, bordering on out-and-out shame, was being critically scrutinized by every eye on the court. After all, she was almost a full-grown woman, except for her pudgy hands, and he was just a little boy with a baby face. His eyes scanned the court again, to make sure no one was watching. It was then that he spotted Benny, who was sitting in the corner and rocking back and forth, as he silently read a small black book that Scotty supposed was some sort of prayer book. Who let *him* off the hook?

Then, with the rip of the needle across a few grooves, and a few short seconds of blessed distortion-free silence, the Israeli dance instruction was over, and everyone retreated to their cabins. Scotty walked the short path, hoping as he walked that there would be no more dance lessons for the rest of that camp year—and doubting the hope. Benny was walking right behind him—so close that if Scotty stopped short, Benny would run into him. Out of Scotty's irritated interior came a thought so loud and clear that it almost seemed audible.

"Is that crazy religious zealot gonna breathe down my neck all summer long? Great."

He increased his pace, just to put some distance between them.

Chapter Five

Three days into Scotty's camp "detention," Shlomo gave every boy in the cabin an on-the-spot assignment to write a post card home. He hand-distributed them to each boy. A photographic collage graced one side of the 4X7 cards, with space for a short note, mailing and return addresses, and a stamp on the other side. The entrance sign of the camp was pictured at the top of the collage side, with a few snapshots of "interest" under it—such as the building housing the *chadar ha-o-chel*, and both an exterior and interior photograph of one of the cabins. Scotty wasn't a fan of either writing or reading long letters—so the size was, like the bear's porridge, just right for him. Everyone was lying on their beds on their stomachs, pens in hand. Scotty's head pivoted to Gus first, then over to Benny, and finally to Brandon. They all seemed quite literary, etching word after word into tiny sentences on their cards. What tomes could they be penning after a mere three days of camp life? Perhaps the fact that Scotty was an only child made the difference. They probably had more people to say hello to. He closed his eyes and took a deep breath for inspiration. Or was it a yawn? Then he began.

Dear Mom and Dad,

He paused. Why did he address his mother first in the few cards he had written? Was it because he was a mama's boy? He wasn't that. Perhaps it was because he wasn't a daddy's boy. No, the truth was, he never had the relationship with his father that he observed in other boys' families. His father was always too consumed with his job as a corporate accountant for a financial company, whatever that was about, to be there for Scotty. He didn't even know what there looked like or felt like. Even if he could have compared his dad to other dads, that thought never even occurred to him, just as it didn't occur to him that his father might read the note he was about to write. He continued to scratch out letters just large enough to keep things short and shallow.

I'm doing fine. The food is okay. We played baseball the other day. I can't remember who won. I have a friend named Brandon. He's nice.

Bye for now,

Scotty

He put down his pen and looked around him once again. Benny was adjusting his yarmulke on his head with one hand and writing with the other, which irritated Scotty.

He's a mama's boy for sure. He's probably telling her what a good boy he's been, saying his prayers while wearing those ridiculous boxes with the Shema prayer in them—as if God sees that.

Scotty was surprised at his cynicism. He wouldn't have used that word…cynicism. Still, the attitude surprised him. He noticed that Gus was finished writing and was headed for the bathroom. Brandon was across the room talking to a boy whose name Scotty had memorized for future use, although he hadn't talked to him yet…Malcolm Berman.

Malcolm was more all-around pink and pudgy than he was out-and-out fat. He was ahead of Scotty when it came to the sensitive area of physical maturity, but not that far ahead. And there was another area where Malcolm was ahead of not only Scott, but everyone else as well. He was rich—that is, his family was well-to-do. Everyone in the cabin knew it, because he seemed to produce one luxury item after another throughout the summer—not the least of which was a sturdy air mattress, so he could camp in comfort after an evening of toasted kosher marshmallows around the campfire—while everyone else slept with their sleeping bags on the stony hard ground.

Scotty couldn't help but notice that Malcolm had something—or more accurately, two somethings—in his hand. Curious, Scotty walked toward him and Brandon.

"What's that, Malcolm?"

He spoke the name confidently, convinced the boy didn't yet know *his* name.

"What do they *look* like, Malnick?"

Apparently, Berman not only knew his name. He also knew his last name. He glanced at the matching items, with their buttons and antennas, and painted camouflage green. He paused, and then took a risky guess.

"Um…walkie-talkies of some sort?"

"Duh. Yeah, that's what they are."

Scotty breathed an almost imperceptible sigh, and then asked the obvious.

"Do they work?"

"Of *course*, they work."

"Right. Cool. Can we try them?"

"What for? Why would we use them now, stupid? They're for camping."

Scotty was stung by Malcolm's put-down. *Who did Berman think he was? Some spoiled rich brat, who gets any expensive toy he wants? Mommy, I want those walkie-talkies! Wah-wah! I want them now! Or no, his mommy probably told him, always have them with you in case you get lost. I wouldn't want my precious baby to get lost and cry for his mommy.*

"Scotty. Scotty. I'm over here."

Brandon was by their beds. Scotty was glad for the way out, and followed suit, leaving Malcolm holding his walkie-talkies to hang out with him.

After dinner at the *chadar ha-o-chel*, Scotty followed everyone—both boys and girls—to the *bay-dam ha-gadol*, the large log cabin-like building housing one large room and bathrooms. White plastic chairs were placed assembly style, facing a plain unfinished pine podium. Behind the podium was a blackboard, but there was nothing written on it.

Shlomo stepped forward, along with the folk-singing counselor, who introduced herself to any clueless boy present—for example, Scotty—as Lilly. Lilly with straight black hair. With her acoustic guitar strapped on like an uzi, she began strumming in some major chord. The rhythm of the song was obviously not in the American folk tradition. It was in more of an oom-pah beat—Germanic, Gypsy, and Jewish all at once.

The lyrics, starting with the word Tzena, were obviously in Hebrew, although Scotty had no idea what they meant. He was likewise unaware of the American recording by folk singer Pete Seeger. Seeger had heard the Israeli pioneers—the *chalutzim*—sing it. He had recorded it in 1949 with the group The Weavers, on one of the first Columbia vinyl long-playing records. And he transformed it into an American Civil Rights protest anthem—along with his own anthem, *We Shall Overcome*. The modern nation of Israel was still young in 1964, the *chalutzim* had imbibed a socialist structure in Russia, and the result of all this enthusiastic idealism was the *Kibbutz*, a sort of Israeli farm where songs like this were sung. Lilly's siren singing voice demanded attention. And Scotty was listening.

After Lilly finally laid her guitar to rest in its open case like a slain civil rights worker, she looked around the room and scanned the earnest idealistic faces of the campers. She took a deep breath and smiled.

"Yours are the faces of the future. Yours are the faces of hope. I stand here amazed at all of you. You will make a difference, each one of you. You will make a better world. Just twenty years after Hitler sought to exterminate the Jewish people, there is still hatred, there is still prejudice, there is still anti-Semitism, there is still racism."

She paused to allow her sober words to soak in, and then continued on a more positive note.

"And then there are young people like yourselves. This summer, all of you will learn the meaning of a special word, a word that is sorely lacking in so many so-called 'good' people who raise their children, work their jobs, and live in their split-level houses with their two-car garages. That word is 'tolerance.' As folk singer Bob Dylan, who wrote that song you've heard me sing, 'Blowin' in the Wind,' also sang last year, 'The Times They Are A-Changin'.' And you are the young people that will change them."

She turned to Shlomo.

"You all know Shlomo here as a counselor at Camp Chalutzim. But did you also know that he spent time in prison last year?"

All eyes shifted to Shlomo. He closed his eyes, smiled, and nodded, as if to say, "I'm guilty."

"Shlomo, do you want to explain yourself?"

"Sure. It's true. I spent two nights on a urine-stained and scented mattress in Mississippi, in the deep South."

Every girl in the room made an "eww" face.

Then Shlomo proceeded to share his experience working as a civil rights worker, alongside Medgar Evers and other blacks and whites, which also included Jews like himself. As he described one particular Woolworth's restaurant sit-in in which he had participated a year earlier in 1963, he instantly rose in Scotty's estimation. His introverted personality had obscured his illustrious adventures, like the dark side of a brilliant silver dollar moon. Now, he told just enough of his lunch counter encounter to at least hint at the violence involved. He did, however, end up exposing his war wound, a usually hidden scar between the hairs at the top of his head, where it was met with an empty beer bottle in mid-flight. At that, the attitude of the girls was transformed from one of rapt attention to one of deep sympathy and teen female admiration. And when he described being present at Evers' assassination, sniffles could be heard to the corners of the room, all of them female.

Scotty quickly looked to his right, left, and behind him to see who was crying. He noticed Sandy at four o'clock on his right, in the row behind him. Her baby blue eyes were awash in tears, which were streaming down her cheeks. He wanted to kiss each tear, in a comforting sort of way. Then he looked forward again, hoping no one was looking at *him*.

When Shlomo was finished, Lilly closed with a song. She lifted her guitar out of its velvet-lined casket-like case, resurrecting it with march-like straight eighth notes.

If I had a hammer, I'd hammer in the morning, I'd hammer in the evening, all over this land. I'd hammer out danger, I'd hammer out warning, I'd hammer out the love between my brothers and my sisters, all over this land.

This was followed by *This little light of mine*. Lilly mentioned that we all have a little light. She said that both Jews and Christians like the martyred Medgar Evers and the very much alive Martin Luther King believe we have a little light that can shine. What little light? Scotty didn't feel any little light inside him. But he *did* feel just plain old little, little like a little boy, and lost in the dark of a lost summer, as he walked back to the cabin and his thin-as-a-pancake mattress.

Chapter Six

Scotty arrived at the cabin just in time to be greeted by a pillow fight. As the screen door slammed behind him, a pillow in mid-air collided head on with his face. Irritated by the anonymous assault, he threw it to the ground. He didn't realize how much the lunch counter account had affected him. The laughter of his bunkmates seemed infused with the sting of Southern segregation. Aching feelings of alienation were quickly being honed into sharp pains of persecution. Even Brandon, who had reached out to him in his loneliness, began giggling and then stopped himself short as if in mid-sneeze.

When the pillows had been sorted out and returned to their respective beds, Shlomo spoke to his war-weary bed-ready soldiers.

"All right. I understand blowing off a bit of steam after those emotional stories. I know reliving them with you affected me. I'm sure they did you as well."

At that exact moment, the sound of taps blared through crackling record grooves and distorted PA speakers. Scotty realized that same sound could be heard throughout the camp, including in Sandy's cabin. And the same ritual of changing from jeans to pajamas was being observed by everyone—counselor and camper, male and female. For Scotty, the art of the pajama quick-change was already wearing as thin as his mattress. And he wasn't any more skilled at it than he was the first night of camp. He looked down at his jeans as he removed them one leg at a time, his t-shirt still draped to his hips. He kept his underpants on. He would change them in the morning, despite his mother's admonition that he should remove them so his changing body could have a chance to develop as he slept. It could develop some other time. He wasn't in the mood to give it room now. Then he slipped between his sheets. He turned his head toward Brandon's bed. Just as the night before, Brandon's flashlight was casting shadows under the tent of his top sheet. Scotty knew he was reading. His curiosity was once again piqued. Why was Brandon being so secretive about his reading material? Not only was he reading undercover, literally. He was also unwilling to answer Scotty's question about what he was reading. Scotty somehow knew he wouldn't be able to sleep until he asked about the book once more. He whispered just loud enough for Brandon to hear.

"Hey Brandon."

He waited.

"Hey Brandon."

"Yeah, what is it?" Marks whispered back.

"What's that you're reading?"

Brandon paused. Then he threw his sheet aside, flashlight still on, and jumped out of bed. He stood next to Scotty's bed, with the closed book in his hand.

"It's a secret. You can't tell anyone."

"Why not?"

"You just can't."

"Why not?"

"Cause."

His hand obscured the book's face.

"Okay, I'll just tell you, it's written by Jews. And it's about…"

He leaned over and whispered in Scotty's ear.

"Stop kidding," Scotty spoke in his regular voice.

"Shh."

"I mean it. Stop kidding," he repeated, this time in a whisper.

"Okay."

Brandon got back in bed. He was beginning to drift off.

"It's not Jewish," Scotty interrupted the silence. There was no answer.

"You'd better not tell Benny." There was still no answer. Brandon was already asleep. Scotty knew where the book was. He had seen Brandon hide it in the middle drawer of his flimsy false walnut fiberboard bureau, under several thin short sleeve shirts. He whispered Brandon's name one last time, just to make sure he was asleep.

"Brandon. Brandon. Hey, Marks."

He crept out of bed and stood still, his eyes checking for the least sign of movement in the colorless grey room. Then his hand reached out in one smooth slow motion, like a slithering serpent, and clenched the book between his thumb and forefinger. He withdrew it in another single motion, until it reached his chest. He turned back to his bed and to his sheets, carefully grabbing his flashlight along the way. Once he was safely inside the tent of his sheet and blanket, he flipped the volume open indiscriminately. It didn't matter to him where his eyes fell, since he wasn't looking for anything in particular. He just wanted to know what about this book seemed so important to Brandon that he would risk being discovered with it, knowing very well it had no place in a Jewish camp.

Let your light so shine before men, that they may see your good works, and glorify your Father which is in heaven.

Scotty's mind instantly connected the words in front of him to music and lyrics he had heard so recently that his mind had played them subconsciously several times over the last few days, like a selection in a

1950s Rock-Ola Juke Box.

> *This little light of mine, I'm gonna let it shine,*
> *This little light of mine, I'm gonna let it shine,*
> *Oh, this little light of mine, I'm gonna let it shine,*
> *Let it shine, all the time, let it shine.*

He could hear Lilly's voice, and the straight-eighth note strumming of her large curved yet boxy acoustic guitar. He figured the words must have come from those verses in the New Testament. He hadn't considered that they might have, and perhaps Lilly never considered that either. But he remembered her saying that both Jews and Christians have this light, so maybe she *had* considered it. Either way, it was of no consequence to him.

He gingerly put the book back in the drawer and under the short sleeve shirts. As he got back in bed, the light shining outside the cabin was switched off. There was no moon or stars that night, due to a cloud cover. There was no *little light* anywhere in the vicinity. Everything was black. So, there was nothing to do but lie there alone until he finally fell asleep.

He was the first one awake in the morning, just as he had been the last one to fall asleep. It was as if he was the only moving thing in an otherwise still picture. Then, like a bloodless battle cry, recorded reveille crackled forth. Within less than a minute, the picture took on motion. Everyone in the cabin was on their feet, and two lines had already begun to form in front of the bathroom doors. Scotty ended up behind Benny, who had already taken his black linen yarmulke off his bureau and placed it squarely on his head. For no rational reason, this irked Scotty, who was already disappointed. He had dreamt of his room, and house, and front yard back home, and then woke up to these barren *barracks*—and to bunkmates like Benny.

This sour attitude—well, sour beyond other mornings that summer—continued beyond the bathroom and dressing. His actions were blank and automatic. And he didn't say a word to anyone. If he were older and more "sophisticated," he might consider himself depressed. But even if that word wasn't in his emotional vocabulary, he knew he wasn't happy. Even if he was up before the others, and hungry for a decent breakfast, he ended up lagging behind as the boys walked the gently sloping hill to the *chadar ha-o-chel*. Only Benny was behind him, walking in his uncoordinated clumsy *yeshiva student* way. Scotty wanted it to stay that way, but for some unknown reason, Benny was in a talkative mood. Scotty could hear Benny's footsteps catching up to his, until they were even with Scotty's. Benny started right in.

"I hope they have blintzes."

Scotty wanted to eat breakfast, not talk about it. So, he changed the subject to something he was more curious about.

"I noticed you sat out during the Israeli dancing yesterday. How'd you pull that off?"

"Geveret Brombeck let me out of it. I'm not supposed to touch girls. My Hebrew School teacher says it's because they might be having their periods."

"Oh."

"You *did* look like you were eating a sour pickle while you were dancing with Bunny. I guess I know why now."

Scotty laughed nervously. Benny elaborated.

"I don't like the Israeli dance time. It's like the goyim. That's the way they are when they do their goyishe dances."

Something about what Benny said, or maybe the way he said it, or both, bothered Scotty. His closest friend in elementary school had been a Gentile named Teddy. He felt like he had to say *something* or he would betray Teddy, even if they were in different classes now.

"I...I don't know. My best friend in sixth grade was a Gentile."

"Best friend?"

"Yeah, best friend."

"Friend, okay. But *best* friend?"

"Is that a problem?"

"Yes, I think so. I wouldn't have a Gentile best friend. I mean, they don't eat kosher, and they don't believe in our God, and…I don't know. *Friend* I can understand. But *best* friend? I don't know."

Scotty stopped short and tugged on Benny's sleeve.

"Yeah, best friend. You got a problem with that?"

"Hey, let me go."

Scotty's emotions were agitated. He'd never had a conversation like this. He wasn't quite sure where to go with it. But he knew he had gone too far when Benny shook his arm off him. But it was too late. Scotty felt a need to defend himself physically, even though he knew even bookish Benny was more a man physically than boyish Scotty. He gave Benny a light shove to the chest with his right palm. Benny shoved back with more action than Scotty expected. Then, like an internal combustion engine operating on all cylinders, a no holds barred boxing match ensued. One punch led to another, until they both ended up on the ground. Benny got the better of Scotty, and was on top, throwing wild punches to Scotty's unprotected chest and stomach. The rest of the boys just stood there, stunned by what they were watching. This wasn't typical behavior at Camp Chalutzim.

Shlomo waved his hands wildly in the air and shouted "l'haf-seek! l'haf-seek! Stop! Stop!" He and Brandon entered the fray, with each one taking a boy, pulling them off each other and back. Shlomo grabbed Benny and Brandon grabbed Scotty, whose spindly arms were struggling against his constricting adolescent grip. By what authority was Brandon stepping into Scotty's business? Scotty wouldn't have phrased it that way. But that was the sense behind his resistance. Shlomo thundered authoritatively again, this time with clear finality.

"Enough!"

Shlomo relaxed his grip even before Benny's struggling ended.

"Both of you, come with me."

He led Scotty and Benny over dirt path, grass, and paved sidewalk, until they reached the brown slat clad administration building just inside the entrance to the camp. He walked up the few steps to the small landing and knocked on the door. A muffled "come in" emanated from the inside. The three entered. The first thing Scotty noted, even before focusing on the desk with the director sitting behind it, were the bookshelves filled with multi-volumed books. They took up all sides of the cedar-walled room. And in the center of this claustrophobic scene was a large walnut desk behind which sat Rabbi Menachem Malmud. He was younger than his name sounded, about forty. And he wore unremarkable yet unavoidable thick black glasses. He looked up and through the lenses, acknowledging Shlomo.

"Good morning."

His eyes then focused to Shlomo's left and right. He paused, waiting for Shlomo to begin.

"Um…Rabbi Malmud…these two boys were fighting with each other. I felt that we should see you about that."

He waited for Rabbi Malmud to give his short lecture, as he had the summer before, and the summer before that. And Rabbi Malmud didn't disappoint.

"So, what happened?"

Benny started.

"He just started hitting me."

"He called my Gentile friend back home names. He said I couldn't be best friends with him because he's not Jewish."

Malmud immediately realized the situation. He addressed each boy in turn.

"I see. Benjamin, Scotty lives in an area that has some Gentiles, and he has a close Gentile friend. Scotty, Benjamin lives in an area that has almost all Jews. Jewish people have learned to live in both kinds of communities. In *this* community, we must learn to live in peace with each other. Jews must learn to get along with each other here and everywhere. So...should Jews fight with Jews? Benjamin?"

He answered quietly in Hebrew.

"Lo."

"You can answer in English."

"No. No...sir."

"And you? Scott?"

"Well...I think sometimes they do...but they shouldn't...I mean, unless it's in self-defense...I believe."

Rabbi Malmud nodded and smiled slightly.

"Yes, self-defense is permissible under Jewish law. Perhaps we've had to learn that over the years, and some other religions haven't had to... as much."

He was referring to New Testament verses on personal pacifism, but neither boy had any idea what he was talking about. They just wanted the meeting to be over as soon as possible. Menachem Malmud finished with a warning.

"Be that as it may, I don't want to see you two in this office again. Do you understand me?"

They both glanced at each other and then nodded.

"Good. The next time, we will call your parents and they will be asked to come and get you. That's all."

Scotty wanted nothing more than for his parents' familiar blue Chevy Impala to arrive and whisk him away from this awful place. But he kept that thought to himself. Shlomo left first, and then the boys followed. When they arrived at breakfast, applause erupted. Apparently, they were perceived as heroes, which didn't sit well with Shlomo.

"That's enough!"

Chapter Seven

Scotty stared at the outside light, which hadn't been switched off yet. He tried to follow just one mosquito as it gravitated erratically around the light source, like a tether ball around a pole. His thoughts were his personal mosquitos, darting in and out, each a sentence fragment. He reviewed the day that was at an end. They had had blintzes for breakfast, just as Benny had predicted. That meal was better than lunch and dinner combined. So that at least was positive. Benny's Brooklyn-tinged orthodox yet unclean sweat still clung to his hands, although he had washed them since. All in all, notwithstanding the blintzes, it hadn't been a great day. And there were many days left, and many nights—like this one.

He looked over at Brandon's flimsy bureau, where the book was. This time, he didn't call his bunkmate's name. Brandon's metronomic snoring was evidence enough that he was asleep. Scotty slipped out of bed, scanning the dark room like a watchtower checking a prisoner's barracks. All was still.

As smoothly as a fishing rod in motion, he opened the drawer, withdrew the book in question, and reeled the catch in to his waiting pajama-clad chest. Then he withdrew his body back under the sanctuary of his bedsheets, grabbing his flashlight in the process.

Once safely tucked in, he clicked on the light and randomly opened the book. He pointed the light at the printed page.

You have heard that it was said, "an eye for an eye and a tooth for a tooth." But I tell you not to resist an evil person. But he who slaps you on the right cheek, turn the other to him also.

Immediately, he thought of his fight with Benny earlier that day. And with it, the thought came to him, *no wonder the Christians hate the Jews so much. With all that cheek turning stuff, they have to take it out on someone.*

It seemed to Scotty that he had figured out why the greatest ongoing conflict in history was *still* ongoing. And if he had figured that out, maybe he could resolve the conflict too. He was actually quite proud of himself for solving such a complicated puzzle with such a simple solution. It was obvious. Everyone should get into a good brawl now and then. With that solution, the Holocaust might never have happened.

He closed the book with the impractical Christian solutions and carefully placed it back in Brandon's bureau exactly where he had left it. With that accomplished, he immediately fell into a deep sleep.

All days at Camp Chalutzim except Saturday lacked any specific identity. Each of the other days was like a slow-motion march through various awkward activities, dotted with embarrassing moments of personal hygiene, toward a nameless evening of staring at the moon, stars, or nothing at all through the screened window. And Saturdays weren't Shabbat breaks. They were marked by an even slower motion stagnation, where even the sometime accompaniment of Motown, California, and Liverpool on Shlomo's AM radio was missing.

Only the after-lunch escape to the *Fortress of Solitude* near the camp's entrance was worth looking forward to. On the second Tuesday, Scotty was once again practicing his solitaire sport, firing plantain weeds a few feet into the waiting patch of tall grass. The announcer in his head was busy calling "balls and strikes." His lips were moving as he softly mumbled his pretend radio personality's comments. Suddenly, an odd awareness overtook him. Someone was watching. Something with four legs and a smooth shiny coat of orange-yellow hair. He stopped and froze. Blood raced through his arteries, driven by the increased speed of his pulse. A noise emanated from the beast. Was it a threatening growl or a friendly greeting? Scotty was alone, with seemingly no help in sight. Thankfully, a wagging tail gave the animal's intentions away.

"Here, boy."

The dog was content to continue wagging, and that was fine with Scotty, who began to turn his head to his left and right. Were they indeed alone? Apparently not. There, not twenty feet from him, was a boy about his age, with short straight straw blonde hair and a sunburnt ruddy face. He was about as thin as a child his age could get, and he wore dungarees that hung on him like a denim curtain from their brass buttoned straps. His eyes were slate grey. They stared at each other like two frozen deer. The boy finally broke the silence.

"Hey."

Even with that word, Scotty could tell he spoke in a rural Pennsylvania accent.

"Hey," Scotty responded.

The boy repeated himself.

"Hey. What you doin'?"

"Nothing. Is this your dog?"

"Not really. He just hangs out around here."

"Oh."

"You from the camp?"

"Yeah. What's his name? The dog, I mean."

"He had an owner a while back, but he moved away and left him. So, he wanders around. The cook Boris gives him scraps. He calls him

Bagel. So, I call him that. I think it's some kind of food he cooks."

Scotty reached out and petted the friendly dog, who responded by enthusiastically licking his hand.

"It's a great name for him."

The boy changed the subject.

"So, what are you doin'?"

"Nothing…well, I was just playing with the grass. Here, I'll show you."

Scotty showed the boy how he *fired* the plantain heads. The boy tried the same thing, and then—not knowing anything about each other, even their names—they began a simple contest to see which of them could shoot farthest. The results were inconclusive, there being no imaginary narrator or umpire.

After the "game," the boy introduced himself.

"Um…I'm Mack…Mack Jonas."

"I'm Scotty. Scotty Malnick."

"Are you a Jew?"

Scotty froze again. He had never been asked that question. He was trying to figure out how to answer politely and yet unapologetically, before cutting off the conversation and leaving.

"*Yes*, that's right. I am."

"My pa says the Jews don't believe in Jesus like we do. We believe He's the Son of God. We go to that church down the road if you turn left at the camp's entrance. The service is Sunday at ten. The pastor always asks us to bring friends."

Scotty hadn't prepared for this theological challenge, or for an invitation to Mack's church—if that's what it was. He was trying to change the subject when Mack asked his next intensely personal religious question.

"Do you believe in Jesus?"

"*No*…*No, I don't!*"

"My pa says the Jews don't believe in Him. They killed Him. And then He arose. That's a fancy way of saying He got up. I guess He fooled the Jews. Anyway, he fixes things around here, and mows the lawn, and takes care of just about everything else."

"Even if those things happened, I don't think Jesus would do something like that."

Puzzled, Mack paused before responding with bold conviction.

"Yes, He *would*. He *did*."

"Did *what*?"

"You know. Arose…on Easter morning."

Scotty responded with a quip to ease the tension.

"No, I mean He wouldn't fix things and mow the lawn."

Mack's hearty peal of laughter ended the intense polemical disputation. Scotty joined in, and before long both were laughing.

"You wanna play again?"

"Sure."

At dinner, Scotty kept Brandon Marks' secret to himself. But he glanced over his way more than once, although they were on opposite sides at either end of the long table. Brandon was laughing with Benny over something they both seemed to think was hysterical. Or maybe it was just one of them, while the other was faking, waiting for the moment when he could slip him the forbidden book—perhaps when they were alone.

No, that wasn't right. Brandon knew the consequences of sharing the content of that book with anyone in the cabin. That's why its deceptive words were even now hidden, lying in wait under several neatly folded shirts. Oh, the secrets those shirts might divulge, if they only could!

At the end of another precious and now wasted summer vacation day, Scotty was once again the only one in the cabin who was wide awake. The snoring orchestra was more or less silent, which was unusual. He hesitated to get out of bed and get that book from under Brandon's shirts.

He was relieved that he had a logical reason to hesitate; not that anything about his curiosity was logical. Against all reason, the book scared him. It seemed to have an autonomous mind, and to relish tempting him to access it—kind of like the plot to a creepy *Twilight Zone* episode. He would forget the book and just try to go to sleep. But try as he might, it wouldn't come easily. He had never tried counting sheep, and he had no desire to now. So, he just allowed his mind to float through the day, until it stopped at a specific point in the conversation with Mack, like the money wheel on *Jeopardy*, which had premiered that spring. Scotty knew he never killed anyone, let alone Jesus. And he was quite sure his grandparents, and their grandparents, and their grandparents, and their grandparents, were just as innocent. Who was that Mack kid to spew that kind of hatred? And he *had* to listen to it. He shouldn't have talked to that ignorant country kid, and he never would again. And furthermore, he wasn't going to look at Brandon's book either. In fact, he realized he should probably tell someone about Brandon. But then he'd have to admit he was looking in Brandon's dresser. So maybe he should just forget it and just go to sleep…which is what he did.

Chapter Eight

Scotty woke up to the sharp clap of Shlomo's hands, which just beat out reveille, waking up every child in the cabin, including Scotty. He longed for more sleep to escape into. But the five-minute snooze alarm feature on his three tube General Electric clock radio was hundreds of miles away, back in his now vacant bedroom. "Oh, come on," "Let me sleep," and some other saltier invectives could be heard from the various cots throughout the room. Shlomo would not be denied.

"Come on! Up! Get up, everyone! Right now!"

He was holding a large pale-yellow sponge in one hand and a blue plastic bucket in the other. Detergent suds protruded from the top like translucent topping on a sundae.

"We have a little job for you all…something to help you work up a nice appetite before breakfast. I want you to experience what anti-Semitism is firsthand. Let's hit the bathrooms and get dressed. We don't want to lag behind the others."

What others?

Scotty had to wait in line behind several toothbrush and toothpaste-armed boys to get into the bathroom. Knowing that others were waiting for him to finish heightened the usual shame and embarrassment.

When everyone was dressed, Shlomo marched them all out into the slowly rising dawn sun. The whole camp was outside, including the girls. Scotty felt more like a little boy among quickly maturing adults than usual. He particularly noticed Sandy's womanly figure, clearly discernible through her bright blue camp tee shirt and loose white Israeli-style shorts.

Shlomo wore a Pittsburgh Pirates baseball cap with his blue camp tee shirt and almost matching blue shorts. With his white socks pulled up almost to his knees and his bucket and sponge in his hands, he could have passed for an inmate who was performing janitorial duties at a home for the mentally handicapped. No one laughed. They'd seen him wear this outfit before. He continued with his announcement.

"All right. Someone defaced the *bay-dam ha-gadol* with anti-Semitic graffiti. They used some kind of black paint. The police are investigating. Our job is to remove the offensive graffiti."

He lifted the bucket.

"We tried this, and it comes off…with a bit of elbow grease."

He led the co-ed group, along with Lilly, to the *bay-dam ha-gadol*. There in large bold sloppy black letters were the words "DIE CHRIST KILLING JEWS." They took up at least a square yard, if not more. And on the ground were two large buckets and several sponges.

"Someone did this during the night. It had to be someone from the surrounding area. Either that, or a camper or campers did this as a prank. If that's the case, the camp will find out and they will be sent home immediately, along with the possibility of charges being filed. If you know anything about this, please speak up about it. All right, let's get started."

The only thing Scotty could think about was his conversation with Mack Jonas. He tried to recall the details. His heart fluttered and his face flushed. He had just been presented with information that might directly point to Mack's father. Or it may have absolutely nothing to do with Mack, his father, or any of Mack's friends. But then again, didn't Mack say his father talked about Jews killing Jesus? There was evidence enough in that one comment to prove Mack's father did this…or maybe Mack himself…or both. Or maybe…maybe even Brandon Marks. Or maybe not. Scotty's mind was in overdrive. He stood paralyzed by his thoughts.

I'm just a kid. I'm too young for this. I don't even have body hair, like the other boys do. I can't accuse my new friend, or his father. I can't. But I also can't just do nothing. I have to tell someone. But who?

"Scotty. What are you doing? Here's a sponge. Let's get with it!"

Shlomo shook his sponge at him. Scotty picked up his own sponge and started scrubbing. The word *indelible* had increased in popularity year by year since Sydney Rosenthal had invented the Magic Marker in 1952. But never in Scotty's limited lifespan was the concept of permanence more applicable than it was on this motionless warm day. The one grace was the soapy water. At least it was cool and wet, like a swimming pool. But that relief was no match for the salty sweat that flowed from the pores of Scotty's face. He looked to his right and left. The other boys' pubescent muscles were flexing easily. Their arms guided their sponges up and down the building's wall with a mechanical flair. And the results were increasingly visible, as opposed to his.

Even the girls were getting better results than Scotty. Sandy was particularly effective. Scotty glanced her way. The anti-Semitic slurs were slowly fading as she scrubbed diligently. He couldn't help but notice her lithe feminine figure—her tight tan legs in those almost military shorts, and her newly budding breasts under her camp tee shirt. He quickly turned away. He had the body of a little child, and she had the body of a grown woman. Nothing made him feel more inferior than that reality. He wondered whether he would always remain a little boy physically, and she would continue to develop to the point where she might as well be his aunt…or even his mother. He refused to allow himself to admit that he liked her. In fact, once or twice he found himself staring at her adorable

Hayley Mills-Mick Jagger face a few seconds too long. He was glad no one seemed to notice. After all, silly little crushes the length of a few days or less tended to dot the summer. One between Gus and Sandy lasted about four days—longer than the typical length. But Scotty knew no one would notice his torch for Sandy. Its light was well hidden beneath his Camp Chalutzim tee shirt and his smoldering sad heart.

That night after taps, Scotty lay there watching the mosquitos orbiting the light outside the screened window. He thought he would fantasize about Sandy, developing a story line in which he told her of his deep love for her, and asking her if she would be his summer crush. But he didn't. Like the mosquitos, his thoughts took orbit. But they were circling a different planet. Instead of Sandy as the sun, the center was Mack's father, whom he had never met, but nevertheless knew more about than he wanted to. Once again, Scotty had to speak to someone about his talk with Mack. After all, Mack's father worked for the camp, right on the property, and may have scribbled the graffiti. *Somebody* did. And Scotty knew just whom he should talk to about it.

Chapter Nine

When Scotty awoke the next morning, Mack's father no longer occupied a primary place in Scotty's thoughts. Instead, Sandy's carefree mouth and generous eyes opened as his did. Her dream-soaked voice spoke the sweet words, "I like you, Scotty…a lot." The "*a lot*" part was more alluring than the "*I like you*" part. That was the vanishing salutation, the *adieu* that left a yearning like the scent of perfume accompanying a soft kiss—not that he had ever experienced that kind of kiss. His first thought was, *what was that about?*

Even though Sandy had trumped the Jonases in Scotty's unconscious mind, he made a now wide-awake choice to confide in someone that very day about Mack Jonas and his father. And that someone was Lilly—straight black-haired folk singer Lilly, who he was sure would want to know about Mack's comments. Over puffy bleached white rolls and papery scrambled eggs, Scotty sat unusually quiet and planned his as yet unscheduled visit with Lilly. It would be short, direct, and all about the prejudiced minds of "carefully taught" Mack Jonas and his Jew-hating father. He raised his eyes from the quickly cooling eggs to check out the "girls'" tables. Sandy was in her usual place. And so was Lilly. He hesitated several times before rising and heading for their table. Brandon and Benny watched him, as did Shlomo, who was wondering why Scotty "crossed the line." He stood next to Lilly and waited for her to finish laughing at something. Sandy noticed him first and grabbed Lilly's attention by pointing toward him. She addressed him as Scotty, which surprised him. They had never talked.

"Yes, Scotty? Can I help you?"

"Um…um…"

He lost his words, like Ralph Kramden of the old *Honeymooners* TV show.

"Um…"

Then, like Queen Esther before the king of Persia, he petitioned for a future meeting.

"Um…um…I was wondering if…if I could talk to you…"

"Now? Here?"

"No. No. Later…today…maybe…about something."

He could hear his bunkmates' loud whispers and giggles.

"What's Scotty doing? Is that his new girlfriend?"

Lilly stayed focused.

"I have some time at three o'clock this afternoon. I can meet you at the *bay-dam ha-gadol*."

It wasn't the most private place for a meeting. But he said yes, hoping they could find a corner in the big room.

"Um…okay."

Scotty spent the time until then in stressful anxiety, through a smashed flat grilled cheese sandwich and watery tomato soup lunch, and then several uncaught outfield balls. When 3:00 pm finally came, he once again hesitated. But he had committed himself, and he knew he had to follow through. When he showed up, she wasn't there. He was relieved, even though it was a short-sighted relief. He was about to leave when Lilly rounded the corner of the wood slat building. At first, she seemed preoccupied with some other business. In fact, she was. She and Shlomo were planning to have a serious talk later that afternoon. But she made an effort to focus and live in the moment, a skill she had been practicing through the last year with the help of a college therapist.

"What's up, Scotty?"

Despite her Zen-like effort, the few words were clipped. Scotty refused to be distracted by her seeming impatience. He had been preparing for this moment, and he would not be deterred.

"Um...I wondered who to tell this to. But...I...I mean *and*...I thought I should tell you...not to tattle on someone, but...so you can help me know what to...to do. It's about the maintenance man...here at Camp Chalutzim. His son Mack is...my age. Sometimes we talk by the front gate. We're even kind of friends."

"He lives around here?"

"Yeah...I mean, yes. Right around here. And...Mack...he told me some things his father told him...about how the Jews killed Jesus and stuff like that. I thought with your singing about the "little light shining" and all, you might just want to know about Mack's father...not to get him in trouble or anything. I just thought you should know."

"Oh. Well, sometimes we just need to tolerate ignorant people, Scotty. But maybe he won't stay ignorant. Maybe, as you and Mack continue to be close friends, he'll see another side of Jewish people than *his* father was taught, probably by his father. That's how prejudice stops. And it's good to have friends who grew up differently than we did. But...I don't understand, Scotty. What does that have to do with the 'This Little Light of Mine' song?"

Scotty looked around him, and then lowered his voice. He hadn't been planning to divulge the secret about the book in the dresser. But knowing he was in the presence of such an open-minded and kind person, he confided information with her that he hadn't shared with anyone else—even Mack.

"Oh, that. The song. Well…there's this boy. His bed is sort of across from mine."

He leaned in closer.

"After everyone goes to sleep, I can see him reading by flashlight under his covers. Later, he puts the book in his dresser, under some short sleeve shirts. Anyway, when he was asleep, I quickly read the part in it about letting your light shine."

"Well, it's good to read before going to sleep. It helps sharpen the mind and settle it down at the same time. But I still don't understand. It's a song. I don't know about any book with that in it."

Scotty hadn't considered that Lilly didn't know the verse about letting your light shine.

"Oh. Well, it's kind of in the Bible…sort of."

Lilly began to scan her academic memory banks for any verses in the Torah, or maybe in those ever-emphatic Jewish Prophets—although she was no Biblical scholar. Still, it sounded familiar. Perhaps it was part of rabbinic commentary. Where had she heard the quote, other than in the song? Then suddenly it came to her. It was in—of all places—a college literature class, over the last year. *The Bible as Literature,* to be exact. And to be more exact, it was in the *Sermon on the Mount,* in the New Testament book of Matthew. She made a turn-on-a-dime decision to smother any surprised response and change the subject—but not before asking one final question.

"Oh, I got you. What was your friend's name again?"

"He's my *best* friend at camp. Brandon. Brandon Marks."

"It's good to make close friends at camp," she threw in, before going back to the initial topic.

"Maybe you shouldn't spend time with that boy. What's his name?"

"Mack?"

"Yes. Mack. There are so many campers your age."

Scotty wasn't sure how to respond. If he ignored Mack, it would hurt him. And he didn't feel right doing that. He decided to drop the subject without another word.

Chapter Ten

Thursday evenings were reserved as movie nights. The whole camp filed into the *bay-dam ha-gadol* and sat down row by row on the long benches. As would be expected, the 10-year-olds were the loudest, but everyone in the room took the opportunity to socialize with their bunkmates. The girls sat with the girls and the boys sat with the boys. Even those going steady ignored their crushes. Taking a boyfriend or girlfriend to the movies or a similar event was fine for home. However, at Camp Chalutzim, dating was not a temporary event. It was a summer long opposite sex selection—a selection as in, *I'm going steady with her,* or *That's my boyfriend.* And everyone understood the two-month nature of the relationship. It ended with that year's summer camp. Any contact off-campus through the year was treated as if it never existed. To put it another way, the romances at Camp Chalutzim had an offshore limit. The "country" of Camp Chalutzim was a two month or so port of call and nothing more.

The movies came in two categories. One consisted of a few sixteen-millimeter reels of old, brittle (the proof was in the periodic snapping) black-and-white Hollywood films. For example, Cecil B. DeMille's 1939 dinosaur *Union Pacific*, about the joining of the east and west railroad lines in the mid-1800s, could be relied upon to put floor-bound crossed legs into a prickly tingling sleep. Once, Benny not only lost his balance when he stood up as the lights came on—he also lost his yarmulke, at least until he retrieved it.

The other category of films could basically be defined as patriotic propaganda material from modern Israeli history—for example the 1948 Israeli War of Independence. These movies were always in Hebrew with English subtitles. And their plots were typically predictable. Some soldiers were always taking a hill tagged with a number—Hill Number Seven, or Hill Number Nine, for example.

However, the film that night was completely different. For one thing, it wasn't about 1800s America, or 1948 Israel. It was, in fact, newsreel footage from just one year before, in August of 1963. There, in focus and yet slightly out of sync, was a man whose name everyone had heard often over the last year—at least on the evening news. Martin Luther King was certainly larger than life, especially in relation to Scotty, who sat "Indian-style" just feet from him. King's imposing visage contrasted boldly with the edges of the white movie screen.

"When all of God's children, black men and white men, Jews and Gentiles, Protestants and Catholics, will be able to join hands and sing in the words of the old Negro spiritual:

'Free at last. Free at last. Thank God Almighty, we are free at last.'"

The only thought that lodged in Scotty's mind was, *Mack and his father should hear this man. They need to hear these words.* This was followed immediately by words he had heard often over that same year, words that described King's work...passive resistance. They allayed at least some of his frankly prejudiced Aunt Sarah's repeated fears about the few "Negro" families that were moving into her all-Jewish neighborhood. At least they wouldn't rise up against her. But then she would invariably wonder out loud whether King was building a monster that would move from passivity to angry aggression.

Just then, those recently learned verses from Brandon Marks' book echoed in Scotty's increasingly agitated mind.

But I tell you not to resist an evil person. But he who slaps you on the right cheek, turn the other to him also.

He wished he'd never read those verses. But after seeing King onscreen, he wondered whether it was actually possible to, as this Jesus of the New Testament recommended, love one's enemy—for example, Mack's father. Once again, he concluded that Jews who did that just ended up dead at the hands of Nazis.

Movie night finally ended. It was time to cease his dizzying thoughts and try to forget the evening's entertainment—if indeed it could be called that. He would intentionally think of something else when he went to bed that night. He hoped it wouldn't be like not thinking of the color red, or green, or white…or *black*. But when the time to sleep came, it ended up being exactly like that. He turned this way and then that, twisting his sheets around him like a full-body tourniquet which restricted the free flow of a pre-dream state and replaced it with obsessive thinking.

Passive resistance, cease and desistance, rabid persistence, repeated insistence, No! Get off of me Mister, give in to your fist sir, slap on the kisser, No! Kiss Sandy's lips, sir. Yes sir, kiss Sandy's lips.

His increasingly unconscious mind settled on Sandy's lips. And in that state, he dreamed. But when he woke up, remembrance of it dissipated like fog's mist giving way to the sun's morning rays. And indeed, the sun was quite strong that morning. The shadows were black, and it was only in those shadows that squinting was unnecessary. None of the campers wore sunglasses, so everyone squinted in the sun. In the ninety-degree heat, sweat dripped from Scotty's forehead and accumulated under his Camp Chalutzim ball cap even in the mountainous surroundings.

That morning's breakfast lay heavy in Scotty's stomach. He wanted to go back to the cabin so he could use the bathroom in total privacy and then lie down for the rest of the morning. But that luxury only existed back home. He had, however, just discovered a "secret" bathroom in the lower level of a large cabin used for some kind of administrative work. He had been on one of his post-lunch "rest" periods when he found it. Like the small respite near the camp entrance, his *Fortress of Solitude*, this hidden treasure would make the summer a bit more bearable. He decided to visit it only in extreme circumstances. Other bathrooms in the cabin and throughout the camp were too public. Here, the sounds and smells of his most private needs would not be detected by anyone else. He glanced around him as he separated from the group and quickened his pace until he arrived at the cabin in question. Two or three female staff members were typing on manual typewriters. He eyed a steaming coffee cup on one of their metal industrial desks. The worker stopped typing to take a sip, and then returned to her percussive work. The stairs to the lower level were just a few steps away. His thoughts "shouted out" insistently.

Don't turn around. Don't turn around.

It was working. So far, they hadn't noticed him. He gingerly sneaked over to and down the stairs on the balls of his feet, tiptoeing in his Keds high-tops. When he got to the bottom, he spied the bathroom door. There was only one bathroom, and there was no designated gender specified. He opened it and then gently closed and locked it. Finally, he was in a truly private bathroom for the first time that summer. He quickly pulled down his pants and underpants and sat on the toilet. Ah, this was the life! Real privacy for the first time! And the toilet paper was so much softer than the sandpaper in the cabin. More like home. He grabbed some toilet paper and began to relieve himself, working as quickly as possible. Just then, he heard what sounded like the click of high heels on the stairs he had just descended.

Oh no!

Someone rapidly knocked on the door while barking the last

question he wanted to hear.

"Who's there?"

It was one of the secretaries, or whatever they were. He had to say something.

"Um…a camper."

"Come out of there!"

"I can't."

"A camper…and a *boy yet!* Well, finish up quickly and get out of there. And don't use this bathroom again!"

For a short second, Scotty wondered whether he was in a *girl's* bathroom. But he knew that wasn't right. He had checked, and he was sure there was no male or female sign. He closed his eyes and held his breath. He didn't have to look in the mirror to know his face was a shade of red deeper than any sunburn.

He heard her clicking heels fade, and the screen door slam. She was gone. He hurried and then got up and pulled his pants up. He wasn't sure which was more embarrassing—this incident, or his hairless boyish body. He knew he would remember this one for the rest of the summer, and maybe for the rest of his life. At least it felt that way. He quickly washed his hands and left. Fortunately, she was nowhere in sight. He knew he couldn't use this bathroom ever again. What a waste of a good private space. He walked back to his cabin in time to lie down on his bed. Brandon was working with his baby shampoo and baby powder clay. Benny was reading something in his prayer book. And Scotty tried to take a quick nap—and failed.

Chapter Eleven

The receding summer sun gradually gave way to a full firmament of stars. Scotty watched a small sample of them through the window. Some twinkled so brilliantly that he half expected one to arrive like Pinocchio's Blue Angel, transforming him back into "home-boy," and his own cozy and private room. He tried to discern a constellation or two through the partial view. He had seen both the Big and the harder to make out Little Dipper, both at camp and at home. But this fragmented exposure yielded neither. It was at least a slight comfort to him that the same stars that shined here shined upon his family's longed-for house. With no further light displays to occupy him, he escaped into a light sleep.

A forgettable dream ended with the arrival of Venus, the morning star. The rising sun wouldn't be far behind it. Scotty looked around to see if by chance anyone else was awake. At first, he concluded that no one was. But then his eyes glanced at Brandon Marks' bed. It was very neatly made up, complete with the hospital corners everyone was taught to fashion from the sheets. But Brandon wasn't there. He could just make out Shlomo on the other side on the room. He was breathing in and out while he lay sleeping on the side farthest from Scotty.

For several minutes, Scotty lay on his back. Then he made a quick decision to use the bathroom before everyone got up. He figured it would be best to get that over with while it was unoccupied, and no one was conscious—no one but Brandon. And he only needed to use one of the two bathrooms. Fortunately, he only had number one to dispatch, and then perhaps he could get some more sleep. He would take care of number two when everyone else was at breakfast.

Gingerly, Scotty sat up and then found his worn corduroy slippers with his bare feet. He slipped them on the wrong feet before switching to the proper ones. He stood up and steadied himself. Then he began to walk by sliding his feet on the floor to avoid any creaking on the polished pine wooden planks. He slowly navigated towards the bathroom. Suddenly, one boy and then another rose from their beds and quickly outwalked Scotty. Meanwhile, his body was expecting to empty its bladder, and the urge was building. This wasn't working. He headed for the cabin door and carefully opened it, paying little attention to the squeaking noise associated with the hinges.

He realized that dew would soak his slippers, but that was a price he had to pay. He walked on the grass and headed for the trees.

I must have had too much bug juice.

He found a conducive tree and relieved himself. Then he prepared to leave. As he turned, he noticed someone or something on a log about twenty or so feet from him. He froze. Then it coughed. *Who wouldn't cough in these wet woods,* came the involuntary thought. It was obviously a camper…and a boy. Perhaps it was Brandon. In a few seconds, confirmation arrived in the form of words.

"I need some help. Could you help me?"

Brandon couldn't be talking to *him.* Or could he be? No. That wasn't possible. Maybe someone else was there.

"You said you would give me wisdom. Well…"

Was he talking to a counselor? At this hour?

"I need it. It's about this kid in my…a bunkmate. Well, you know who it is. He doesn't seem happy. Maybe it's homesickness. I try to talk to him, and…well, he seems like he's somewhere else. You know, in Proverbs, where it says there's a friend that sticks closer than a brother? I didn't want to come here this year, but if I make friends with some of the guys, that makes it a bit better. I think he could use that too. Anyway, they don't know about You…or us. I can't tell them now. I hope You understand. I'm not ashamed or anything. I'm just…lonely. So…I can't handle that just yet. You know, the rejection. Not yet."

Scotty guessed Brandon must be talking to God, or Jesus, or whatever. He had never heard extemporaneous prayer. It didn't seem Jewish, or even right. Maybe it was disrespectful. Or maybe God wanted someone to talk to. *Really* talk to. If He really *was* there, maybe He was lonely too…like Scotty.

He hadn't been back in his bed a half hour when the familiar recording of reveille simultaneously vibrated outdoor speaker cones throughout the campus. This was followed by the unexpected vibration of an indoor speaker cone electronically connected to Shlomo's blonde fabric suitcase phonograph. Shlomo clapped his hands a few times as the arm stylus found and then melodically navigated the wavy grooves.

"Good Morning, Good Day. How are you this beautiful day? Isn't this a beautiful morning? Very."

Shlomo stayed up with the very latest Broadway musical comedics. Not that he had ever actually been to one. But he *had* been to a few roadshows soon after they left Broadway. And he had an impressive collection of original-cast 33 1/3 RPM vinyl albums, which he coddled and cradled like newborns. Sheldon Harnick and Jerry Bock would introduce their masterpiece *Fiddler on the Roof* in just two months, that September. But in July of 1964, *She Loves Me* was their current hit on Broadway, ever since its debut in 1963. And Shlomo played the first song just about every other morning.

"Good Morning, Good Day."

When the song was over, Shlomo lifted the arm and put the record safely back in its sleeve. Then he addressed the campers as they began to line up at one of the two bathrooms.

"This morning after prayer and breakfast, Rabbi Malmud will visit with us in the *bay-dam ha-gadol* about an important matter. So go directly there."

If Scotty had been feeling the exhausting effect of sleep deficit, it now disappeared in a sudden jolt of nervous apprehension. What was this about? Had "the book" been discovered? Was Brandon Marks in trouble? And consequently, was he, Scotty, in trouble? He davened more quickly than usual, weaving to-and-fro and forward and back as if he was the star of his own private silent film. He would have eaten just as quickly if he had eaten at all. But he ended up playing with his food, and then laying his utensils down on his plate.

Thirty minutes later, every boy and girl bar or bat mitzvah age or older was seated cross-legged on the pine floor of the *bay-dam ha-gadol*. Shlomo and Lilly stood in front with other counselors from the cabins up to four years beyond Scotty's age. Rabbi Malmud was by her side, along with a middle-aged policeman who could have been described as fit, except for a small beer belly that hung just above his belt.

The younger campers were noticeably absent, having left for their morning classes. If it weren't for the volume of the socializing in the hall, it might have been possible to hear them in the distance. But as it was, any one of the younger campers would need a bullhorn to be heard. Shlomo clapped his hands sharply several times and shouted "Shecket! Shecket! Quiet! Quiet!" Silence slowly overtook the room as if someone was turning down the volume of a three-tube amplifier. Lilly took that as a cue to start.

"We won't keep you long. It's a sunny day, and I'm sure you want to get out in it at some point. Rabbi Malmud just has a few words to share with you before that. So please give him your attention. Rabbi?"

The rabbi stepped before them, his newly sun-freckled face having gained a few more of them over the last week or so.

"As Lilly here just mentioned, I know you all want to get your day started. I just want to introduce Officer Clark from the community police department. Please show him the respect he deserves by paying attention to what he says. Officer?"

Clark stood there, legs parted and hands on his hips like an umpire behind home plate. He had an accent that was an indefinable mix of small-town urban, suburban rural, and a touch of regimented military.

"All right. At ease. At ease."

Scotty's eyes darted from one boy to the next, as did Brandon's and a few others. It seemed to them that they were already as much at ease as they could possibly be.

"All right. I won't take much of your time. I just want you all to be on the lookout for whomever it may be that wrote those words on that wall there…the one you all cleaned up so well…which I personally thank you for."

The compliment was followed by a firmer tone.

"This police department doesn't tolerate that kind of behavior," he barked as if he was accusing *them*. "Writing graffiti is a misdemeanor, which would remain on your presently pure and pretty records. And when said offense includes hate speech like that, it could rise to the level of a *felony*, which might just mean jail time for the joker who perpetrated this despicable act!"

He paused as his eyes scanned the room. His investigatory skills had been partially on autopilot, and yet at the same time open to the remote possibility that one of these young Jews was pulling a fast one on the ever-vigilant law enforcement personnel.

When Officer Clark's eyes met Scotty's, they bore into his like an industrial laser. Did the cop have prior knowledge of Mack Jonas and his Jew-hating father? Was Scotty withholding relevant information related to an actual crime? Was blood on his hands? And what about Brandon Marks and his Christian book? At least Scotty had come forward and told Lilly about that. And hopefully, things would end there. Hopefully, Brandon's secret would go no further. After all, it was just a book. And it wasn't like it was pornography. Lilly hadn't seemed upset. In addition, he had heard that some Jews study it as literature in high school. He knew that colleges did. Even his older cousin did. Hopefully, everything would be okay now. *Hopefully.*

Chapter Twelve

The gossip grapevine at Camp Chalutzim spread like the measles… or perhaps more like mononucleosis, also known as The Kissing Disease. Gus and Sandy broke up on the third Sunday evening after dance class. By the next morning, news had reached the farthest cabin, like news of Beatlemania had crossed the Atlantic days before their first appearance on the Ed Sullivan Show. And in both cases, the female members of the species were responsible for the super-spread.

That day after lunch, Scotty retreated to his *Fortress of Solitude* and the sport of Plantain Heads. He had just matched his all-time distance record. Bagel was there as a witness, like an umpire. Scotty sat on a log, satisfied with his victory. Suddenly, he could sense an approaching presence that he just knew was a fellow camper. He knew instinctively that it was a *girl!* He could tell by the feminine stride. He turned around just as Sandy's tousled almost-blonde hair and full baby blue eyes approached him. She was wearing her Camp Chalutzim tee shirt and pink shorts. His eyes focused on where her belly button would be. A combination of stark fear and frightening attraction jump-started his heart. The only thing that came to his overwhelmed mind was, *what do I do now?* But he didn't need to worry about what came next.

Sandy lowered herself straight down like an elevator, until their eyes met. The next two things that came to his mind were, *Oh my, I haven't taken a shower for two days,* along with *I hope she doesn't realize what a little boy I am.* She came close and cradled the back of his head. Then she spoke for the first time.

"You are *so* cute. You're adorable. And I really like you."

As Bagel circled them, tail wagging, Sandy brushed her lips against his for a passionless second. Her eyes widened.

"Ooh. I love how you kiss. I *really* like you. Let's go steady."

He wondered what he did that she loved so much. But he had to say something, especially since the most beautiful girl at Camp Chalutzim had just kissed him…sort of.

"Okay."

Then, just like that, it was over. But by dinner, he was the new subject of female gossip in every cabin in their age group and the next.

The next morning, the new king and queen sat with their own cabins at breakfast, as usual. But a discerning eye would quickly catch the new seating arrangements. The distance between the two freshly minted lovebirds had been shortened to the closest proximity that simple geometry would allow. And Sandy, at ten-minute intervals, walked over to the table where Scotty was sitting in front of his papery scrambled eggs. Everyone who entered the *chadar ha-o-chel* noticed the magnetic duo. They were now the most popular couple in the camp.

All the boys at camp had a hierarchy of popularity among them, and Scotty was nowhere near the top. Sandy, however, was in their view a 9 out of 10 in looks, with the aforementioned Mick Jagger hair and Hayley Mills face. And in terms of the potentially devastating "personality wind chill index" that might lower her overall score as it had so many self-possessed girls, that was rather low. So, she was well within the margin of error, and a real catch in any guy's book.

The other summer bonus for fortunate attached couples was hand holding. This was very new for thirteen-year-olds, and the staff at the camp knew it. They had a responsibility to the offsite mothers and fathers to keep their hormone-saturated adolescents from exploring each other's freshly discovered bodies. The solution was to keep them occupied with camp activities. But like hounds in heat, they were adept at finding spaces like the one frequented after lunch by Scotty—his *Fortress of Solitude*. Things also worked well during slow walks back to the cabins on moonless or cloudy nights. Couples would pair off for a few short minutes. They would invariably end with closing in—and then finally that passionless kiss.

Scotty had just finished a particularly uncomfortable late-night hand holding walk home with Sandy. It was hot and more humid than usual for the Pocono Mountains. His hands were dry, but hers were sweaty. This dynamic provided a new opportunity for the embarrassment Scotty had experienced without letup all summer. Sandy was just as embarrassed, but neither wanted to offend the other by withdrawing their hand. Silence added to the discomfort. Silence, except for the crickets. They produced more of a racket than a romantic setting.

When the couple arrived at Sandy's cabin, Scotty could just make out the dim outline of a few pajama-clad girls through the screen window. They seemed to be almost pressing up against it. Scotty made the peck even shorter than usual.

"Hey," came a whisper. "Have a good time?"

Sandy shot a whisper back.

"You should have been there."

"I'll bet."

Another voice chimed in.

"Oh, he's *so* cute. Hi, Scotty."

Now Sandy had something to prove. She pulled Scotty against her and gave him the first real kiss either of them had ever experienced. It started as a show-off kiss, but it didn't stay there. She locked onto his lips and kept on kissing until she was out of breath. Scotty was too embarrassed to loosen up and passionately kiss her back. Still, he was enjoying it as much as she was. Then she turned away from him and toward them.

"So there!"

A mature woman's voice emanated from inside the cabin. It was Lilly.

"Girls! Get in your beds! Sandy! Get in here! And Scott! Get out of here and go to bed!"

Scotty left. When he arrived at his cabin, he wasn't greeted with the same interest that he and Sandy were in front of her cabin. In fact, everyone in Scotty's cabin was fast asleep. Everyone, that is, except Brandon Marks. He was under his covers, with the flashlight beam bobbing around as he read *that* book. *Let your light shine,* it said in that one place. At least that Scotty knew, he was the only one who was aware of the book Brandon read undercovers by the beam of his flashlight.

Later that night, when he was once again the only one awake, Scotty was tempted to take the book from Brandon's dresser again. But the risk was too high. As it was, some of the boys were tossing and turning on their flat hard mattresses. At any rate, he decided that it wouldn't be right to read a book that wasn't meant for him. Maybe it was meant for Christians like Mack's father, who didn't like Jews. But it wasn't meant for him. *Let them try to love their enemies,* he scoffed as he remembered the words Jesus said in there. *I can't even imagine what it would be like to love someone who just wants to be mean all the time.*

Just before dawn, Scotty woke up and experienced his worst case of homesickness yet. Of all things, he missed his mother's hugs most. She had an unmistakably unconditional way of hugging him. When she did that, he would get a picture of her holding him as a very little boy. He could see in his mind's eye his toddler's corduroy-clad legs dangling, as her arm supported his little behind, and he rested his head against her chest. He would get that picture every time she hugged him. And he missed those hugs most. Second to that was her meatballs and spaghetti. Nothing at Camp Chalutzim even came close.

In the morning, Scotty couldn't remember any of his dreams. He could only recall thinking of his mother's meatballs and spaghetti. His lonely heart ached as he contemplated the bland breakfast ahead of him. Whether it was fake scrambled eggs, or wilted waffles, or whatever it was, it all reminded him that he wasn't home. He wasn't in his own bed. He wasn't in his own backyard. And this wasn't his real and *true* life.

Chapter Thirteen

Scotty first heard about the three rabbis from Shlomo. The news came in the form of a joke he told to Lilly, which was overheard by Scotty, who wouldn't have understood it if it hadn't been for Christmas. But since no one in America could avoid the Luke 2 account—even if the source *was* A Charlie Brown Christmas—Scotty got the quip.

"Well, you got the three wise men to drive here tonight all the way from Harrisburg."

"It's only fifteen miles."

"By the North Star."

Lilly smiled and gave Shlomo a knowing look.

Nothing more was mentioned until after the post-dinner prayers, the melodious *Birkat Hamazon* that were chanted directly after dessert— which on this night happened to be a non-dairy pudding that religious Jews could eat with either milk or meat. Keeping milk and meat dishes separate occupied the kitchen staff throughout the summer.

The three wise men happened in this case to be three rabbis in black suits with white starched shirts. One was middle aged, with a graying beard and a generous belly, and wore a black brimmed hat. The two that accompanied him were younger, clean-shaven, and thin, with black silk yarmulkes. One had short red hair and the other had short dark brown hair. The three sat quietly eating by themselves, occupying three chairs next to each other as they chanted the Birkat Hamazon.

When the prayers after the meal were concluded, the entire camp, from bar and bat mitzvah age and up, were told there was a special assembly in the *bay-dam ha-gadol*. Each age group was led by their counselors out of the *chadar ha-o-chel* and directed to the meeting hall structure. The normally noisy campers were quieted by curiosity. They filed in and sat on the floor in the places usually reserved for movie nights. Lilly walked up and stood before them. Scotty, who would not normally notice such things, could detect a stressful intensity in Lilly's eyes. She wrung her hands. Then she began.

"Attention. Attention."

The quiet campers focused on her earnest face.

"We have three distinguished rabbis from Harrisburg. They have asked for a few minutes of your time. I have explained to them…"

She glanced their way and then back.

"…that we are…are very open minded at Camp Chalutzim, and tolerant of people from different backgrounds. We Jews have historically been a tolerant and open-minded people. We read and evaluate for ourselves, based on our historic sense of justice, truth, and mercy."

She was obviously counting herself among the open minded.

"However, there is an appropriate time and place for everything. These rabbis asked if they could come help us separate the appropriate time and place from the inappropriate time and place."

No one within the sound of her voice had the slightest idea what she was talking about…not even Scotty. Then, the rabbi with the short red hair stepped forward. He seemed sterner than the other two. His eyes scanned the crowd robotically. Then he focused on an indistinct point beyond any of them.

"As Jews, we have suffered much at the hands of others. I know you have all studied these things in Hebrew School. It's a very tragic history. As a part of this history among the nations, the so-called holy books of these people have been used by them to cause us great harm. They are not meant for us, and we are forbidden by the rabbis to read them."

Neither Scotty nor any of the other campers had ever heard anything like this before. Their Jewish education had been liberal, and no reading material was off limits except perhaps pornography. And even that was mostly left up to parents. Brandon Marks began to tremble, which Scotty noticed.

"The so-called New Testament is forbidden for Jews," the rabbi stated forcefully. "It has no place at this camp. Whoever has one in their possession must bring it to the main office. As I said, it has…"

Lilly held up her right hand and interrupted.

"Hold on, Rabbi. *Wait* a minute! When you asked to speak with us, I thought you would share something about our history. I didn't expect you to ban books, no matter *what* was in them!"

What followed approximated arguments Scotty had witnessed between his father and his older brothers throughout his childhood. The rabbis had thick Eastern European accents, whereas his father had lost much of his. But it came back during those occasions. Those were some of Scotty's most painful memories. Their hands would fly high up in the air and then all around them like an octopus's tentacles, as the pace of their heated words increased, along with their volume. This argument generated similar heat. Lilly upped the temperature, her face turning red.

"I'm embarrassed I asked you here. You are unread ignoramuses, each of you!"

The red-haired rabbi stoked the fire further.

"You…you should not even mention that rotten book in the innocent ears of these Jewish children!"

Lilly had had enough.

"These children are taught to ask questions, not shut the world out. This meeting is over!"

"So, whose book is this?"

"I said, this meeting is over!"

"I will find out, and the one who allowed this will be disciplined, and maybe worse! Such a *shanda* in a Jewish camp! Such a disgrace!"

Shlomo hadn't said a word, which bothered Lilly. He tended to take time to gather his thoughts, so that he could maximize his ability to defuse and even resolve crises. He saw it as an application of rabbinic wisdom, but often it came off more as cautious disengagement. Lilly saw it as abandonment in her time of need. She was becoming increasingly frustrated, especially with Shlomo.

"Shlomo, say something. Please!"

Finally, Shlomo, in an effort to defuse things, spoke in an intentionally calm voice.

"I'm sure Rabbi Malmud would allow literature like this, as long as it's not used to proselytize."

"Don't be so sure!" the older rabbi shot back anything but calmly. "At any rate, we'll find out. If no one else speaks to him, I will! It's a *shanda!* That's what it is."

There was a pause lasting two or three beats. It seemed that no one wanted to continue the meeting except the red-haired rabbi, whose agitation had not abated. He was expecting a clear and final decision about the existence of a New Testament at camp. But Shlomo had advised against banning it. So, it seemed a meeting with Rabbi Malmud was the only answer. The meeting with the rabbis ended with that expectation, and everyone went back to their cabins by the light of a clear starry night.

Chapter Fourteen

The next morning, Scotty slept late. Every camper overslept. It took several seconds for Scotty to realize there had been no reveille, and no accompanying rallying cry from Shlomo. The sky was lighter, and the sun was higher, beyond the window frame—as if, like a child's yellow helium balloon, it had floated away and taken the dawn with it.

Shlomo stood next to the screen door like a sentry, with arms at his sides. A few boys were already headed for the bathroom. The line began to grow with campers whose bathroom schedule had been thrown off. Scotty hadn't even joined it yet. Fortunately, he had gone in privacy before the sun came up, while everyone else was still asleep. He pitied the boys who had to wait in line. But he still had the challenge of the clothes quick-change to endure. Shlomo stood amidst the brown metal bedframes, drab-green blankets, and pancake-thin mattresses, with arms now folded like a marine sergeant.

"Okay, sleepyheads. Welcome to 8:00 am. You can daven your Shacharit prayers in the cabin. There are siddurim over here by me... unless you have your own to chant and pray from."

"What's going on?" Brandon blurted out. Shlomo kept his answer short and to the point.

"Some idiot vandals made a mess of the *chadar ha-o-chel*, tore up some screens, broke a few windows. It's nothing that can't be fixed, but not before breakfast."

A cacophony of voices shouted questions at Shlomo. Scotty didn't need to know any more about what happened. He was *sure* Mack's father had something to do with it, and maybe even Mack himself. He hoped he'd never see Mack again, at the *Fortress of Solitude* or anywhere else.

Red haired freckle-faced Gus Simmons had something to say about breakfast, which was all that was on his mind.

"So, are you gonna let us starve?"

That triggered a "break-fast, break-fast, break-fast" chant, while everyone banged rhythmically on their bedframes in time with the chant, like jailed convicts in an old gangster film. Shlomo raised his palms.

"Enough! *Zeh Dai!* You guys are privileged. You'll get breakfast in bed. Now pray before it comes and gets cold!"

That calmed the prison population, which settled into prayer, led by Shlomo, who stood in front of them facing forward. When that finally ended, breakfast arrived. It consisted of quickly cooling rolls and sealed 8 oz. cups of orange juice. A roll fight would have erupted if everyone wasn't so hungry.

Later, after morning conversational Hebrew studies, box lunches came to the cabin the same way. Walking from class back to the cabin, the boys passed a crew repairing screens, removing and replacing broken glass windows, and cleaning up the shattered glass. Scotty was sure the vandalism had to be the work of Mack, or his father, or both. The "devastation" was too great for just *one* vandal. But he hesitated to accuse his camp-entrance friend—let alone his father—without clear evidence. And even if there *was* clear evidence, he wondered if he would still have kept that evidence to himself.

After lunch, the break ended up being even longer than usual, due to the in-house meal. Everyone decided to just stay inside or stand around outside the cabin for the hour or so before the usual planned baseball game. Everyone, that is, except Scotty, who was suffering his worst bout of homesickness yet. Unmissed, he quietly walked away from the cabin, his hands stuffed into the pockets of his blue jeans. He followed his restless feet as they took him past other cabins. He felt as close to depressed as a thirteen-year-old in his position could feel, like a lost and lonely refugee far from the familiar warmth of his home. A meandering country two-lane highway stretched away from the camp and beyond the horizon line for what he knew were hundreds of silent miles.

As he stopped just outside Sandy's presently vacant cabin, he could just see the fence line which surrounded the perimeter of the camp. Cole Porter's lyrics to a song he knew nothing about, except that he once watched singing cowboy Roy Rogers sing it in a movie, entered his mind. *Don't fence me in.* Why should he be corralled like a sad young stallion in this claustrophobic camp? Wasn't this a "free country"? And that being so, wasn't he free to walk wherever he wished, at least within reasonable limits? He longed to walk all the way home, to his own bedroom, and his own soft spring-supported mattress. As he stood and stared at the stained pine siding beneath screen windows, a loud female voice pierced the stillness.

"Scott! Scott Malnick! What are you doing outside the girls' cabin?"

He shut his eyes and muttered.

"Nothing."

He felt for sure he was being accused by one of the female counselors of being a Peeping Tom.

"I'm...just...I don't know..."

"You don't know what?"

"I'm just standing here thinking."

"Well, think somewhere else!"

He began to take offense. Did she think he was a pervert?

"There's no one even in there."

"I don't care. You shouldn't be hanging out here *anytime*. Daytime. Nighttime. *Anytime*."

Scotty got the message, which was along the lines of Lilly's late-night reprimand. But Sandy Singer had nothing to do with his present location. He might as well be trapped in one of the two cabin bathrooms, with the entire camp waiting outside. Shame followed him everywhere he went at Camp Chalutzim. He was exposed, revealed, naked, from the *chadar ha-o-chel* to the *bay-dam ha-gadol*, to the front gate, and even to the *Fortress of Solitude*—a solitude which Mack and his father disrupted periodically.

After just a few weeks, Scotty began to approach each day's activities with somber and depressing acceptance. When Shlomo stood before the boys at the end of the post-lunch break and announced an impending soccer game, he might as well have been preparing troops for a military battle—at least as far as Scotty was concerned. He had never played soccer. He had heard boys talk about it. The way they described it made it sound like something akin to barely controlled roughhousing. A few of the boys had battle scars, and each scar had a story behind it. Apparently, kicks were the primary cause of injury, and they were gleefully scored alongside the points that determined the winning and losing team. Scotty was about to perform his oft-practiced disappearing act when Shlomo shut down that possibility in a few words.

"Boys, everyone is required to play soccer. It's the national sports pastime of Israel, and *everyone* will participate."

Scotty was sure those words were spoken for his benefit, as well as perhaps one or two others. Within five minutes, everyone was headed to the soccer field. Scotty knew it was a sports field. After all, it had goal posts. At first, he thought it was dedicated to good old American football, in which he had no interest. Now he realized that its true purpose was an even more unfamiliar and uninteresting game.

Of course, the first order of business in any camp sport was always choosing the two teams. And just as in baseball, Shlomo oversaw that excruciating experience. Once that was over, everyone took to the field. He should have been thankful that he wasn't a goalie. At least he wouldn't be pushed, kicked, and even slapped around. Fortunately, those coveted positions—at least in the eyes of most boys—were quickly decided up front. As usual, he was one of the last to be chosen.

Then someone on the team got the bright idea to encourage Scotty to get in there and kick the ball from the center spot. Everyone gave him an enthusiastic pat on the back, including Shlomo. Scotty had no interest in being the man of the hour, or *any* hour. It had to be a joke. But he wasn't laughing because the laugh was obviously on him. He expected the next few seconds to seem like an eternity, but they were over in an instant. Someone kicked the ball from the center spot. Someone else kicked Scotty in the shin and then the crotch. He doubled over in the kind of pain that felt like going under the knife without an anesthetic. Then he went unconscious.

Chapter Fifteen

When Scotty came to, he was in a white room. The floors were white, the walls were white, the ceiling was white, and the door at the far side of the room was white. He was lying in a bed with white sheets and a white pillow. The young doctor at the foot of his bed, however, was dressed in jeans and a Camp Chalutzim tee shirt. The only medical giveaway was the stethoscope obscuring part of the words "Camp" and "Chalutzim."

Scotty took in the whole room of half occupied beds. Then his head turned left and right. A younger boy was on his left and an older boy on his right. The doctor glanced at a clipboard in his hands, and then up. Scotty was so absorbed in his surroundings that the consistent pain he was feeling in his knee and lower abdomen only then registered.

"You took quite a hit."

"Um…I think I got whacked by something…or someone."

"Yes, I heard. You're a conscientious sportsman."

Scotty declined to correct the record. The good physician moved next to him and pulled the sheet aside. Scotty was still in his tee shirt and shorts.

"Just unbutton and unzip your shorts. You can leave your underwear on."

Scotty obeyed, grateful for at least a minimum of modesty in an otherwise public facility. But even that modesty was short-lived. The doctor moved everything aside to check things out, including Scotty's aching testicles. The other boys tried to look elsewhere.

"Hmm. It's all there," he joked.

Scotty wasn't in the mood for stand-up comedy, especially at his expense and surrounded by camper-patients.

"You'll live. The dispensary will bring six aspirin. Two now, two at bedtime, and two in the morning."

The doctor moved on, as doctors usually do. In this case, he checked the younger boy in the next bed. He didn't ask him to disrobe or probe any part of his body. He just moved close to the boy's face.

"We're keeping in close contact with your parents, Billy, and you should be able to join your bunkmates again soon. The blood levels are looking pretty good. Then it's off to the treatment center again. Dr. Gilmore tells me you're a brave boy, Billy. I can see that."

Scotty could tell the compliment wasn't a joke in this case. The boy named Billy responded almost militarily, with a hint of defeatist surrender.

"Yes sir, Dr. Joe."

So, this Billy knew the doctor's name. Apparently, he had seen him before. As the doctor started to leave, Scotty caught his attention.

"So how long will I be here?"

"You can go now. Just take it easy for the next day or two."

Scotty was disappointed. He was just beginning to get used to more private, or at least semi-private, surroundings. The mattress was thicker, the pillow fluffier, and the sheets crisper. Those amenities were a welcome change, even though they were temporary. But the lack of modesty situation was the same here as in the cabin. In fact, it was worse. No one else was dressing or undressing, so every eye of every boy was on him. He got out of bed and began to remove his camp clothes from the white bureau next to the bed. At least he had his underwear on to barely obscure the obvious pre-pubescent reality. He took off his pajamas and slipped into his camp clothes as quickly as possible. Then he said goodbye to boys he barely had a chance to say hello to.

"Well…I wish I could stay longer. It's better in here than it is in the cabins. And I bet the food's better too."

"Not really," Billy retorted.

He glanced Billy's way. It was the first time he was able to get a good look at him. He wasn't exactly bald, but he was closer to it than a brand-new marine in boot camp—except that he was nowhere near as healthy. And he had a strange rash consisting of small red bumps on his arms and legs. Scotty had tried to ignore it.

"Well…get better, everyone."

He said that even though he wished that he hadn't gotten better so quickly. Then he threw in Billy's name, because he wished *he* would get better. And he smiled ever so slightly.

"Billy."

When Scotty stepped into the mid-summer sun, only Gus Simmons' boxy freckled face was there with a friendly grin. He gave Scotty a not quite gentle slap on the shoulder, and then thought better of it.

"Oh…sorry. Are you sore there?"

Scotty smiled back.

"No. It was in a more private place."

"Ouch! You okay now?"

"Yeah, I'm fine. But I don't think this young kid in there is. He looks like death warmed over if you'll excuse the expression."

"Oh. I think I know who you mean."

"I don't think so. He's like three years younger than us. Maybe more. Something seems really wrong."

"Yeah, that must be him. My mother knows his mother. His name is Billy Bitner."

"Really."

"Yeah. I know him."

"Does he have a rash type of thing? That's what this kid has."

"Yeah. That's right. He's got some kind of blood disease. Luke something, I think she said it was called. It's a longer word, like four syllables. It's a cancer of some sort. His mother told my mother that she wants him to experience life while he can. Something like that."

Scotty whispered in response, as if his words were adding weight to an existing curse.

"Really? Like he's gonna die or something?"

"Well…I think so. Maybe even like this school year."

That came out wrong, like it was juicy news. So, Gus tempered it with his mother's strict advice.

"I'm not supposed to talk to anyone about it."

"Oh."

Just then, a cold tingling chill swept from Scotty's neck down his spine, ending in a thud somewhere between his stomach and his small intestine. He had never been around any child who had died, was going to die, or even might die. Even his deceased grandparents expired before he was born. But someone his age, or even younger? Silence like death itself generated a stillness like the void in a vacuum. His breath having temporarily left him, there was nothing more he could say. The thought that Billy would be beneath the ground in a coffin by the next summer brought on a spiritual vertigo. Scotty rudely walked away without so much as a "bye."

Back at the cabin and in the land of the living, even if it was in his mind uneasy living, he resorted to making and molding baby powder-shampoo clay with Brandon Marks. After moments of morbid silence, he decided he needed to tell someone about Billy Bitner, and it might as well be Brandon.

"So, this kid in the infirmary, he's got cancer of some kind."

Brandon turned to him.

"I know someone who was healed of that."

"Really? I think it's pretty rare for that to happen."

Brandon didn't mean to share those words, let alone the next ones. They just poured out like spilt milk.

"Well, a lot of people prayed."

"Oh."

There was an awkward several seconds. Brandon wasn't sure how to clean up the "mess" he'd just created.

"Well, maybe someone here at camp could pray a...a prayer or something."

Scotty forced out a stiff and short response.

"Sure. I guess so."

He shaped the "clay" into a ball and added a crude nose. He would have added the eyes and mouth, but it was time for dinner.

Chapter Sixteen

The evening meal started pretty much as a liturgical and culinary replication of every evening meal that summer, with the short Motzi (*He brings forth*, as in bread) prayer in the beginning and the much longer melodious *Birkat Hamazon* (blessing for the food) prayer at the end. Scotty knew the Hebrew almost by heart, but he wasn't sure what the translation meant, other than the "Blessed are you, Lord our God" part. For instance, he didn't know that it contains a prayer to break the yoke of exile off Israel's neck, leading her to her own land, to her own home. Had he realized that's what it meant, he might have shouted an enthusiastic "Amen!" Exile described Scotty's summer perfectly. So, what was so blessed about whatever god was responsible for him ending up stuck here in this lonely place?

These thoughts would have remained safely tucked away in Scotty's personal mental vault if he didn't end up uttering a few fragments in the hearing of Jesus follower Brandon and Orthodox Benny. Like his earlier thoughts, his musings escaped his lips as the overflow of an afterthought.

"Oh, my goodness. Why do we have to say this *every time?*"

Brandon didn't expect Scotty to say that about prayer. But a normally subdued boy named Henry Dreyfus, whose French Jewish parents had each survived the worst indignities imaginable in Auschwitz, and then met in a displaced persons camp after the war, found his voice after Scotty's short sentence.

"You know what? It *is* a colossal joke. Everyone here but the religious fanatics with their yarmulkes glued to their naïve heads knows there is no such thing as God."

That got Benny's attention.

"Shut your blasphemous mouth, Dreyfus."

"It's a free country, Benny boy."

"This is a Jewish camp!"

"So was Auschwitz!"

Benny, the studious yeshiva bocher, was now in his second fight. Only this time it wasn't with Scotty. It was with survivor's son Henry Dreyfus. And this one looked like it would be to the finish. Every boy around the tables was now surrounding the two boys as they both fell to the floor and began wildly kicking and punching each other. Everyone just naturally chose their side, as if there were bets out. The shouting could be heard all the way to the camp offices.

"Come on, Benny. Beat him to a pulp!"

"Get him, Henry. Fight for free speech! Freedom of religion, and even *from* religion!"

That skeptic's mindset had originated in the mouth of the camper's Reform Jewish parent, who had no clue that their son's fellow camper was, at that very moment, in a do-or-die fist fight with the son of Holocaust survivors. Shlomo had every expectation of restraining his passive *Civil Rights worker* tendencies and diving right into the middle of the maelstrom to end it. But during his short few seconds of hesitation, stocky, red-faced camp cook Boris burst out of the kitchen like a gunslinger through swinging saloon doors. His thick Eastern European accent and the concentration camp number tattooed on his arm indicated that he had seen much fiercer fights than this one. He approached them and grabbed each of their Camp Chalutzim tee shirt sleeves with his meaty hands. Benny's yarmulke had fallen on the ground. He wanted to grab it so his head would be covered before the Holy One, especially with the remnants of the lunch he had blessed still in his mouth. But that wasn't possible.

"You boys, you stop! What you doing? You are Jews! Jews don't fight Jews! As a Jew, I know this!"

The boys' faces were still red with rage. Shlomo was glad for the cook's help.

"Thank you, Boris. Now boys, you apologize to one another."

The boys just stood there, averting their eyes.

"Come on."

In response to Boris, Henry reached his hand out first. He could do no less, what with Boris having endured suffering not unlike his parents', who had similar tattoos from Auschwitz. The hand remained extended, hanging in midair for what seemed like minutes. But it was actually about seven seconds. After a very short shake, the fighters withdrew their hands.

That night, back at the cabin, everyone could see that the episode bothered Henry. Benny, however, seemed unfazed by his two bouts. It didn't even occur to him to analyze the encounters beyond a conclusion that "good" Jews suffer at the hands of others, including "not so good" Jews. Henry, on the other hand, had just read the 1954 novel *The Lord of the Flies* in English class that year. And the discussion on its theme wasn't lost on him. In fact, it impacted him deeply. The boys in the book reverted to savage behavior in their relationships. But the parents shared the same tendencies, as the father's appearance at the end of the book emphasized. He turns out to be a military man, playing out the same destructive behavior in his adult world. Henry couldn't help thinking that he carried a mark not unlike his survivor parents, although invisible. It was a mark of the Nazi curse, the twisted burning brand from hell. And he felt like he would never be free from its effects—not for the rest of his life.

After lights out, Scotty couldn't sleep. Benny and Henry were both snoring in an odd arrhythmic pattern. Perhaps they were locked in unconscious auditory combat, the leftover dregs from the grapes of that day's wrath. Then suddenly, the auditory scene changed to another location, outside the cabin, somewhere at the edges or just outside the camp. First a woman's high-pitched voice, shouting and even screaming, then the loud piercing cry of a dog's desperate whine. Then something like firecrackers. At least that's what they sounded like to Scotty. Then an even more desperate whine. Finally, the peace of that summer's night momentarily returned, only to be violently interrupted by an increasingly piercing siren, joined by another, and the clanging of a fire engine bell. By this time, everyone in the cabin, and the whole camp, was either sitting up in bed or standing. Shlomo let the cabin screen door slam shut as he walked out barefoot in his pajamas. He looked back toward the roused campers.

"Stay here."

He stood on the wet grass several feet from the door, watching other counselors stream out of their cabins in similar manner. Boris stood between cabins like a sentry, the full moon reflecting on his almost bald scalp through his thinning hair. A police car pulled into the camp, its siren winding down as only vehicle sirens can. Two policemen, two fire fighters, and two ambulance drivers jumped out of the vehicles. As Scotty watched them through the screen door, he wondered if the loud pops he heard were the sound of guns. He'd never heard that sound live, only in TV shows. And they didn't sound like pops. But why would this emergency vehicle show up, if the sounds were just firecrackers or some other benign thing?

Rabbi Malmud appeared on the grassy "no man's land" between the girls' and boys' cabins, fully dressed in a bright red short-sleeved dress shirt and tan dress pants, like he'd never gone to sleep and had just come back from a night on the town.

"Everyone, get back to bed. There's nothing to be concerned about."

He seemed very anxious for everyone to obey, just as every camper was anxious to see who screamed. No one made the first move. They all just sat or stood there, as if they were staging a silent protest, demanding an explanation. Brandon was the first to break the silence.

"What are they hiding from us?"

Henry hazarded a guess.

"I think it's Bagel."

Scotty had just made a new "friend" that made Camp Chalutzim a little more bearable. And now it seemed like even that friend was being taken away…or worse.

Rabbi Malmud repeated his plea.

"You'll find out tomorrow. Go to sleep."

Chapter Seventeen

When, after a restless night, tomorrow came, it began just like all the others, at least for Scotty—as one day closer to freedom, like X's on a prisoner's concrete wall calendar. But by breakfast, he could sense that something was different. Boris didn't come out of the kitchen even once. When the doors swung open with older campers whose rotational duties included carrying trays of breakfast food, he could be seen sitting on his stool with his head in his hands. From her vantage point at the breakfast table, Lilly watched the doors open and close every few seconds, like a motion picture projector shutter. They exposed a grieving Boris sitting in various painful awkward poses. She got up and walked through the swinging doors, placing her hand on his shoulder.

"Have you heard anything?"

Boris didn't lift his head.

"No, ma'am, I have not. I am waiting for the veterinary hospital to call the kitchen. I am much too old for this. Even though it is dog like the ones I have seen roaming the streets of the old country, still this dog was blessing to Camp Chalutzim. Someone who hates this camp wanted to curse the Jews this way."

"I don't know. Maybe it's just neighborhood kids fooling with guns they shouldn't have in their possession."

"That's how it started in my country. Brown Shirts. Hitler Youth. Future murderers. I have seen. I have seen. It can be here too."

Lilly bent over and kissed him on the forehead.

"The camp authorities will keep you safe, Boris. They will keep us all safe."

Scotty watched Boris's face. His eyes, which had closed, now opened to reveal a new and moist gentleness. Perhaps the memories of his late mother had been evoked by the protective Lilly. Parents become more and more transient as children mature into adulthood—until they devolve into memories like framed photographs and words on headstones. But in the case of a Holocaust survivor like Boris, no headstone exists—only grieving. Scotty was surprisingly immersed in what he clearly sensed was a sad tender moment. In fact, he was so immersed that he didn't recognize romantic signals being emitted from a very oddly matched couple.

Benny had staked his slightly distanced claim with, of all the girls in the camp—Sandy! And she was letting every camper in the *chadar ha-o-chel* know that she was reciprocating. For one thing, she was wearing a summery sheer garment, long-sleeved and covering her bare arms. This hot morning, that was a sign of orthodoxy, which Sandy clearly wasn't—normally. In addition, Benny was paper-thin close to her. That was as different for him as the garment was for her.

So, what was in it for Sandy? Was Benny exotically attractive, with his fringes hinting at the *tallit katan* clinging to his not quite yet masculine frame? Whatever was going on, Scotty didn't like it. Even under-cover New Testament reading Brandon Marks bothered Scotty less, although not much less. He had enough of this *odd couple*. It was time to play hooky from Hebrew class and retreat to his own *Fortress of Solitude*, without Sandy Singer, Brandon Marks, Mack Jonas, or even Bagel.

When Scotty arrived at the Fortress, he was relieved to see that it was, indeed, a solitary place—at least on this day. But his relief was fickle and transitory. A deep and narrow crevice of melancholy began to squeeze in on him, with jagged entrapping edges exposing raw emotion. The emotion in turn forced silent tears out of his eyes, which surprised him. And his breathing became shallow and labored, something he'd never experienced before. What was that all about? Perhaps it was the depression adults always talk about. Suddenly, he felt a strange dizziness, which was another unusual feeling. The camp around him didn't so much spin as it floated, like a feather caught in the gentle vortex of a summer breeze. He had no choice but to collapse to a sitting position on the patchy grass.

He had never asked the *big questions*. If he had, perhaps he wouldn't feel this way. What was he doing on Planet Earth? Why was he born into a Jewish home, into a tiny minority of the world's teeming population? And why in the United States of America instead of in some Nazi occupied country during World War Two. Of course, he knew the story of his father's passage to America as a boy. But couldn't his father just as well have been left behind like his cousins in the picture on the mantle, who viewed the world through eyes that looked exactly like his? They suffered the fate of the camps—starvation, ugly shaved heads and skeletal death, and the ash-filled ovens. What made Scotty's father any better than them, or Scotty for that matter? Nothing.

He never wanted to ask those questions or answer them. That was probably because he was too afraid to stand in the direct pathway of his father's rage—lest he accept guilt for being alive—for *just* being alive. So, he didn't ask them. He was an American first. Then he was a Jew. And then he was a late bloomer, and consequently an awkward clumsy boy and a terrible athlete. The childish imaginary game of shooting plantains would have to substitute for runs batted in and sliding into home. And for all he knew, he would be a late bloomer all his life, with no hair on his face or anywhere else. A shameful freak.

As Scotty began to rise from the ground, he heard familiar voices. Instantly, he retreated to a prone position, lying perfectly still like Bagel playing dead.

"Where's that crazy kid? He's gonna be in *real* trouble. I can tell you that."

It was Shlomo, and he didn't seem happy. Lilly didn't either.

"We better find him fast, or *we'll* be the ones in trouble…with Malmud."

"Who cares about Mr. Right Wing Fanatic Senator Barry Goldwater-loving Malmud?"

"The buck stops with us, Shlomo."

"Don't worry. He'll show up."

Scotty felt like an escaped felon. It was excruciatingly obvious his life was not his own. He desperately wished he could just spend quiet mornings alone—apart from Benny, Sandy, Brandon, Gus, and everyone else who in any way intruded on his precious personal space.

Finally, Shlomo and Lilly left. Scotty waited another minute or so in case they returned or someone else showed up. Then he slowly got up and sprinted back to the cabin. First, he took advantage of the privacy to use the bathroom. That increasingly challenging feat having been accomplished, he then flopped onto his cot. He knew he'd used up his trips to the infirmary, at least for now. But he could at least stay here and claim a stomachache upon discovery. But after today, he had no idea how he would get through the rest of the summer, any more than a felon would survive on the cell block.

Chapter Eighteen

Mack Jonas' family lived about a half mile from Camp Chalutzim, in a small one-story house with unwashed white wood slat siding and a partly worn black shingle roof. His father Robert occupied the den more than any other room in the tiny abode, even the bedroom. The one small fifteen-inch rabbit-eared (one was broken) television occupied the same space on its flimsy tubular stand, and constantly emitted audio from its humble speaker, and video from the screen's dull shades of flickering gray. Robert wasn't sure news anchor Walter Cronkite was the "most trusted man in America." But if his words "That's the way it is" suited everyone else, he figured they probably suited him too, until there was a reason to doubt them.

Mack's mother Tricia's musical tastes could be described in two words—Lawrence Welk. The same couldn't be said of Mack's eleven-year-old sister Margaret, whose musical tastes could be summed up in three words—Beatles, Hermits, Stones—in that order.

Mack was a red-blooded American Beach Boys fan. Brian Wilson was no Peter Noone's Herman, at least to the fawning girls. But his stateside pedigree spoke in his favor, at least more than his pudgy pompadour appearance. Robert's statement was a Four Freshmen crewcut. Dinner that night revealed his typical eating habits, including shoveling large mouthfuls of whatever Tricia was serving up in her flowery malt shop style dress—a garment which reached the height of its popularity in the last decade. Her long blonde hair was pulled back and held in place by a thick red band, Ann-Margret style, exposing her smooth shiny suntanned forehead. Just as Robert finished swallowing his latest bite, he turned to Mack.

"When in that busy schedule of hanging out around the camp are you going to cut the lawn?"

"I was thinking tomorrow."

"That would be good. It keeps growing and you keep putting it off."

"I'll do it tomorrow. I made a nice friend…at the camp. A kid around my age. We've been hanging out."

"A Jew?"

"Yes. A Jewish boy named Scott."

"What kind of a Jew is named Scott?"

"That's his name. Scotty."

"Hmm. Shouldn't he be sticking with his own kind? What's he doing spending time with you?"

"He just is. He seems lonely. He wanders down near the camp's entrance after lunch. That's where we met."

"Don't get in trouble with those elders at the camp. It's their camp, not yours or mine."

"Elders? It's not a church, Dad."

"There are *some* kind of Elders among them…of Zion, I think. I read about it."

"I think they call them counselors, Dad. They don't call them elders."

"I don't care *what* they call them. Don't get mixed up in anything and get yourself in trouble."

Mack tried to lose his patience respectfully.

"Please, Dad. I just talk to him during their lunch break."

Tricia weighed in.

"Robert, I'm sure he's a nice boy. There's no harm here."

Margaret turned to Mack and grinned.

"Is he cute?"

"Yes, Margaret. I think you would say he's cute."

Margaret grinned wider before taking in some mashed potatoes. Conversation after that was sparse straight through the cherry pie. As Tricia left the table and entered the compact but efficient kitchen to get Robert's nightly cup of coffee, he turned to Mack and spoke in a quietly emphatic voice just out of Tricia's range.

"You are not meeting with this Jew again. His filthy rich parents didn't spend their bank full of money to send him to that camp only for him to end up spending time with my Christian son. Do you understand?"

Silence reigned as Margaret stared at her black and white saddle shoes under the table. When Tricia returned from the kitchen, Robert put up his hands and then quickly stared at each of his children, unmistakably indicating the topic was off the table...for now.

Mack spent the next day doing everything he could to avoid the *Fortress of Solitude*—and Scotty. Brandon Marks, however, wandered down there after lunch in what was a dry breezy day typical of the Pocono Mountain barometric cycle. There, sunning himself on a patch of weedy grass, was Bagel. Startled, he gave a short yelp and dragged himself up, standing wobbly on his wounded and bandaged leg. Next to him, like Huck Finn on a steamy Hannibal, Missouri day, was, sure enough, a jeans and ball cap clad Scotty. Brandon was slightly irritated that the Fortress was occupied. He was, of course, aware that Scotty often frequented the coveted location, but he didn't own it. Bagel barked declaratively. Scotty turned around.

"Hey."

"Hey."

"You wanna shoot plantains? I'll show you how."

"No thanks."

"You sure? It's pretty cool."

"I saw you doing that with that kid Mack from around here."

Scotty felt the old little-boy shame creep back into his not-quite-adolescent body consciousness. How many of his power hitting RBI campmates had seen him play the silly childish game? And how many campers were laughing about it with each other behind his back?

"Well…I was just being nice to the little boy. I want him to get to know what Jews are really like. You know what I mean?"

"Yeah, well, I guess so. But…he's not so little. He's taller than you are."

That was the most painful observation of all, and it left Scotty speechless. Brandon continued.

"Anyway, he seems like a nice kid."

For some reason he didn't fully grasp, Scotty felt compelled to add a comment about Mack's earlier remarks to him.

"Yeah. He is. But he told me that the Jews killed Jesus. He learned it from his father."

After an awkward pause, Brandon responded with a few clipped words.

"Well…I don't think…he understands."

"Maybe…maybe he understands what he's been taught."

Brandon hesitated, and then got the brilliant thought to quote Lilly's song with the New Testament quote.

"Well…Lilly sings about it, about the little light."

"I know that's in the Bible, their Bible. I read it."

He didn't mention that he read it in Brandon's New Testament, by flashlight in the middle of the night, while Brandon was sleeping. He added, "But it's just a folk song."

Brandon didn't want to argue the point further, so he dropped the subject. Bagel hobbled off, as if the conversation was too much for his doggie ears. Or maybe it just bored him. That was Scotty's cue to wander back to the cabins.

"Well, I guess I'll be headed back."

"Yeah, me too."

Brandon couldn't see the tears that began to fill Scotty's eyes. The old loneliness saturated the silent breeze around him. It seemed as if the summer had just gotten longer.

Chapter Nineteen

Only an ancient siren could woo Sandy away from exotically observant Benny Kahn. That siren was none other than the *muse* commonly referred to as rock and roll. And in the pop-infused summer of 1964 the very ether permeating the camp was replete with it. Interpreted through the thumpy banged out incorrectly fingered piano chords of Henry Dreyfus, it emanated from the *bay-dam ha-gadol* during late afternoon breaks just before dinner.

It took a humorous turn on singing sensation The Four Seasons for the next candidate to "seduce" Sandy during the one season Camp Chalutzim convened. The song in question was "Sherry." It wasn't their latest hit. "Rag Doll" was, having been released in June. But Sandy was no rag doll, and two-syllabled Sandy with an "S" perfectly matched two-syllabled Sherry. So, it was perfect for teasing—although Sandy didn't take it that way. She actually enjoyed the attention, especially from camper-pianist Henry Dreyfus, who was all too willing to substitute Sandy for Sherry during his piano-vocal rendition. And that one musical act marked the end of the Benny Kahn-Sandy Singer affair.

As if to punctuate—if not celebrate—the affair's end, Henry followed this parody with an anthem proclaiming his conquest, the recent

"She Loves You." And to further punctuate the demise, the echoing sound of a series of staccato shots tore through camp. By this time, the camp's personnel knew where the blasts were coming from. That included Rabbi Malmud, who had no desire to confront the family living right off the property. But he knew something needed to be done.

Malmud's staff had already asked twice for a resolution. But he had been hesitant to confront an armed right-wing redneck from the "hills" of Northeastern Pennsylvania. However, with the last burst of sporadic gunfire, he knew he had to act. He picked up his phone, flipped through his Rolodex, and called a number in Philadelphia. He was trying to reach a law firm he had used when he first took his present position. They weren't cheap. But he had an idea that would hopefully reduce the price.

"Hello? Um…this is Rabbi Menachem Malmud, calling from Camp Chalutzim in the Pocono Mountains…Yes, Pocono. Northeastern Pennsylvania. A children's camp. I know a lawyer there. We've used him before. Um…Attorney Mark Cowen. I see. Well, this is time sensitive. Sure. I'll wait."

He tapped an irregular rhythm on his desk with the pencil between his fingers. A minute went by. Two. Three. Four. Finally, a male voice with a thick Philadelphia accent picked up.

"Yes, Mark. It's been a while. How's the family? Good. Good. I'm doing as well as can be expected, considering this swamp of papers on my desk and the kids I'm responsible for, for another few weeks or so. Listen. I've got a very big favor to ask you. If you can take an afternoon and come up here, I'll make it good. If your kids can come up here for camp next summer, it's on the house. And it's the best Jewish education they'll ever get. I understand. Well, sure, ask Marion. But for right now, I can use your help. Tomorrow? You don't know how much that means to me. 2:00 PM good? Great."

He hung up and sighed with a smile. The next day couldn't come soon enough. Rabbi Malmud's office was outfitted for just such meetings. He spent the day struggling to concentrate on anything else besides dealing with the menace next door. He contacted Shlomo and Lilly and asked them to attend. He realized he was under stress. He hardly ate any dinner. That night he had a difficult time sleeping. The next morning, he reviewed his notes and obsessively straightened out the mess that was his desk. Finally, at 2:00, he looked out the window to see Mark drive up and park his car. Shlomo and Lilly arrived on foot a few minutes later. He walked outside.

"Well, thank you for coming from Philly, Mark. Come on in, everyone. Can I get anyone anything? Water, Coke? I can heat up some coffee."

Everyone having declined, he offered each a chair. Then he leaned back in his dark tan leather executive chair and propped his summer sneakers on his cluttered desk. A thin layer of camp dust and dirt coated the soles. Rabbi Malmud began.

"I appreciate my legal friend making the long drive from Philly. That's a lot to ask of you. Like I told you on the phone, I could just use your legal expertise. I'll cut to the chase. We've got a next-door neighbor, so to speak. He's obviously a gun enthusiast. So…he engages in target practice."

Mark, the fast-spoken lawyer with the thick Philly accent, jumped in.

"Well, Rabbi Malmud, it's a matter of second amendment rights versus Scranton, Pennsylvania legal codes affecting the area immediately surrounding the children's camp you have here. And it also has to do with appropriate times for target practice and such activities."

The rabbi couldn't conceal his heated irritation.

"What the f…I mean, what the h…"

He hesitated to use either word.

"Look. First off, this was quite a bit after sunset, to use Shabbat language…that is, Sabbath talk. Way after, any day of the week. And even if it wasn't, even if it was at high noon, this is a children's camp. It's not appropriate at any time, frankly within earshot of the camp, if that were possible. But short of that, it should be kept as far away as the law permits. Isn't there a shooting range somewhere a safe distance from here?"

"I can have my law office look into these matters."

The rabbi tensed as he responded to his friend.

"Couldn't something be done now?"

A short pause was followed by a terse response.

"These things take time to research, Rabbi, with all due respect."

Lilly could see that the original intent of the meeting was dissolving.

"Could we get to the point? Someone needs to just go over there and tell this man that he has to stop firing his gun off."

Shlomo wanted to play the protector's role, which he believed Lilly expected. But her eyes never communicated that message by meeting his. And he was frankly hesitant to stand between an armed hothead—and possible anti-Semite—and Camp Chalutzim. Sure, he had marched with a group of civil rights activists, and had even spent a few nights in an Alabama jail. But even with all of that training in non-violence, he wasn't presently in the mood to get hit by a lunatic—with or without striking back. Lilly, however, had no such hesitations.

"Oh, my *goodness*. I'll go and confront this guy."

Shlomo wanted to save the situation, and his relationship with Lilly.

"I'll come with you."

She finally looked at him for the first time, and her gaze made him feel pitiful.

"Don't bother."

Mark interjected, "I don't think that's the wisest way to handle this…legally."

Lilly was sick of dealing with these insipid men.

"Forget legality!"

She abruptly got up and walked out the screen door, which punctuated her frustration with a spring-loaded bang. Shlomo rose and watched her as she stomped across the field toward the camp's entrance.

"I think she's headed toward Robert Jonas' house."

Rabbi Malmud, eyes closed, quietly and melodically responded.

"I wouldn't doubt it."

Mark repeated himself.

"Not wise. Not wise at all, Rabbi."

"Well, we knew she was a can-do person when we hired her."

Lilly's insistent knock could be heard all the way to the office, as could the creaking screen door as it opened. She disappeared inside.

Shlomo found his voice.

"Should we go over there?"

Mark quickly shot back.

"Absolutely not! Let her make her own mess...for now."

Once inside the Jonas cabin, Lilly was struck by its spareness. The only decoration on its walls was a frame with a dark blue threaded embroidery on an off-white tight knit background. It said, with Protestant spareness, *Welcome to Our Home Away from Home.* That seemed reasonable, seeing that this was, indeed, their home. And above the frame, cradled menacingly in a horizontal rack, was the rifle in question.

There were a few dishes drying on a towel by the kitchen sink. And the living room was just as spare—just two threadbare but intact stuffed and recently occupied chairs facing the small portable television with the one broken antenna. Seeing a television seemed odd to Lilly. She hadn't seen one all summer. But this was, after all, their home.

Lilly began with a simple enough introduction.

"Thank you for letting me into your home. Um...I'm Lilly. I work at the...at the camp, as I'm sure you know."

"Yes, of course we know that," Robert growled.

Tricia stepped in with a softer approach.

"It's good to have you in our home, Lilly. I've enjoyed hearing your wonderful singing voice and guitar playing from time to time, even from here."

Tricia's gracious compliment helped calm Lilly. At least *she* seemed friendly.

"Well…thank you so much."

"Would you like something to eat or drink? We have some nice things that aren't camp food, if you know what I mean. Some nice homemade cookies."

"Oh, thank you, but…"

Robert took another opportunity.

"They're not *Kosher* enough, probably."

"Oh, no. It's not that. I'm not…I mean…"

"You're not a Jew?"

He prepared to challenge that preposterous assumption.

"No. I mean yes. What I mean to say is, no. It's not that. I could eat the cookies. I would eat them, but I'm not hungry. I just came to ask you to…to consider not firing your rifle after lights out. You see…the children are trying to sleep and…"

She had already decided not to challenge him about the gun altogether. She wanted to, but she was hoping the lawyer would be able to work on that. She just wasn't sure what a man with a gun on the wall might do if she told him she was uncomfortable with him firing it period. Fortunately, Tricia stepped in and saved the day…or at least this one night.

"I told Robert the nighttime is no time to fire that thing, even at the target and with extreme safety, what with the camp in the vicinity. Didn't I, Robert?"

Robert didn't have a chance to contradict before she said, "Yes, I did."

"I have every right to fire it anytime, you know. It's constitutional. Revolutionary war soldiers around here fired them all hours of the day and night, and *that's* how we got our freedom. And no Jews…"

He paused for at least three or four seconds.

"…or, or Christians…can take that right away. But…I suppose if the Mrs. says so, I'll do my shooting in the daytime. You know, you don't get as good as I am without practice."

"I'm sure you're very good. Very *very* good," Lilly squeezed out. With those words, the present crisis was averted. They all bid a cordial goodbye. When Lilly left, Tricia spoke softly.

"She's a lovely girl. She'll make a good wife someday."

Robert shook his head as if to disagree.

"If you say so."

She watched as Lilly walked from the Jonas house back to Rabbi Malmud's office. When she arrived, she simply said, "It'll be okay. No shooting at night."

She turned to Mark.

"Maybe you can deal with the day. And you all owe me big time."

Then she left before any other questions could be asked.

Chapter Twenty

The slippery alliteration in the name Billy Bitner facilitated its spread throughout Camp Chalutzim, or at least the cabins whose campers' ages reached back a few years before or forward a few years beyond Billy's ten years. That included everyone Scotty's age—Brandon, Sandy, Gus, everyone. Gus decided it was time to ditch his mother's advice to keep Billy's condition a secret. That was old news, and old news was in the public domain. He wouldn't have expressed it that way, but the logic of the concept remained.

The next step in the irrationally adolescent mind of Gus Simmons was the timeless device of young teen upward mobility—meanness. After some creative thought, he came up with a nickname for *Billy Bitner*—a clever moniker that, to quote Hamlet, was pronounced trippingly on the tongue—Billy Sickner. By breakfast the next day, everyone had heard the name. The serious condition of the target inhibited its direct use when addressing him. But like everyone else, Billy had heard it "through the grapevine." Gladys Knight's musical popularization of that old phrase was a few years away. But the emotional pain inflicted on Billy was right on time.

It didn't take long before the "clever phrase" reached Lilly's ears, then Shlomo's, and finally Rabbi Malmud's. This time, the rabbi decided to leave the office with the cluttered desk to visit the *bay-dam ha-gadol*. He held an informal meeting that included Shlomo, Lilly, and several other counselors, including the counselor over Billy's cabin, Chaim Lipschitz—a young Orthodox idealist with a gentle demeanor and training in social work. Malmud began the meeting.

"Some information has come my way concerning…"

He tried to fix his eyes on no one in particular.

"…concerning some…some particularly unfunny remarks, unbefitting a Jewish camp, and in fact Jews in general, let alone all decent people. There are children in your care, Mr. Lipschitz, that are involved."

He let that sink in as his eyes quickly panned the room like a sharply focused camera lens, while his neck operated smoothly like a fluid tripod. He wanted to mentally document every reaction. Had any of these camp workers heard the cruel remarks? He chose to address that directly.

"I'm talking, to be specific, about Billy Bitner, a child in your cabin, Mr. Lipschitz. Have you heard anything from your boys, or any of the boys at the camp?"

His gaze quickly panned Lipschitz's way. Lipschitz realized he was obligated to tell what he knew. However, he applied wisdom gleaned from the Biblical Egyptian midwives, as well as Rahab from the book of Joshua.

"I can't say exactly…that is, I have no direct evidence. I mean, not directly."

"Please tell me the truth. Has there been, or has there not been?"

"I mean, one boy mentioned something in my hearing. Um…not a boy in my cabin, mind you. I believe it was Brandon Marks who said something…about prayer…from Shlomo's cabin. Nothing more than that. Just about prayer…for the Bitner boy."

"*Prayer?*"

"Yes."

"What kind of prayer?"

"Well...Jewish prayer, I suppose."

"You're sure about that?"

"I...wasn't there."

"Hmm. Alright. Well, *somebody* used the term *Sickner*. Perhaps Brandon Marks?"

"I don't know."

"Well, we'll find out eventually."

Shlomo was aware that the person of interest wasn't Brandon, but was instead Gus Simmons. However, he decided on the spot that he would speak to Gus privately. No one was going to question one of his boys before he did. It was as simple as that. He, in fact, realized he had not one, but two boys to question. He decided to start with Gus. He remembered hearing during his sophomore year in psych class that the best time to reach a child's conscience is at bedtime.

That evening, he waited until taps' mournful blow, and then approached Gus' bed. His eyes were closed, but he couldn't have gone to sleep that quickly. Shlomo leaned over and whispered in his ear.

"Gus."

He waited, and then repeated the name.

"Gus."

Gus, whose freckles were barely visible in the dark, opened his eyes.

"Yeah?"

"I think your joke may have gotten back to Billy Bitner. I mean, I know it did. And I think it may have hurt him. That is, I'm sure it did."

The crickets provided the only response.

"Do you think it did, Gus?"

Gus could only see the ghostly colorless form of Shlomo's features. His eyes were barely detectable, but even in the dark, they were clearly focused on Gus'. He waited patiently for Gus to respond. After what seemed like five minutes but was more like forty seconds, Gus spoke in a faint whisper, so no one who happened to still be awake would hear his cursory confession.

"Well, I guess."

"I'm glad you agree with me. I want you to apologize to him tomorrow."

There was another pause.

"Do you understand?"

"Yeah."

"Well, okay. Good night."

How could Gus ever get back to sleep, knowing such a humiliating fate awaited him. He realized he would probably have to go up to Billy in the *chadar ha-o-chel* during breakfast. He was sure someone else must have laughed at the "joke," or at least grinned. And then perhaps he spread the word. Was it Scotty Malnick? No, he was too shy. He always seemed so embarrassed, with his little boy looks. Gus noticed how he hid from everyone in the shower. He never seemed to want to call attention to himself...except that one time when he and Benny got into it. And he was always wandering off somewhere. Was it Brandon Marks? No, he was always reading that New Testament he hid in his bureau drawer. Everyone knew it was there. It was amazing that they hadn't taken it away from him. And what about Benny? No, Benny was too serious to crack jokes like that. It couldn't be him.

By the next dawn, Gus' obsessive process of elimination dissolved like the evaporating dew beneath the rising sun. Nevertheless, with the sunrise came his impending execution—to be specific, his execution of the responsibility to apologize to Billy Bitner. He had no idea what he would say. That didn't matter to him. He just wanted to get the whole thing over with.

When breakfast was almost over and it was just about time for the Keetah Hebrew lessons, Gus hoped all was forgotten, if not forgiven. Like the dew, or a quickly forgotten dream, the prospect of a public apology seemed to dissipate. But like the wet grass soaking unsuspecting feet, or a quickly fragmenting nightmare still haunting the conscience, the apology still hung in the thick morning air. Shlomo wrung the words out of Gus' sweaty, strained conscience.

"Gus."

"Yeah?"

"Well? I'm waiting."

Gus paused, and then searched for words that had not yet gathered as thoughts. He turned to Billy and focused somewhere between his eyebrows and forehead.

"Well…well…seeing that you're sick…I mean seriously like *no hope sick*…I'm sorry I called you Billy Sickner."

There was silence deader than the prognosis. Then, while Billy was beginning to tear up under the impact of the thoughtless words, a jittery nervous laugh escaped traditional Orthodox Benny's mouth—of all the campers in the room. And like an infection, it spread to at least three tables, including Sandy's. Even Brandon Marks giggled, which surprised those near him. Then it quickly ended with a loud table-bang, skillfully executed by Shlomo.

"Zeh Dai!" he shouted in Hebrew. "That's enough!" And that was enough. Breakfast was over. And so was all conversation about Billy Bitner—for now.

Chapter Twenty-One

Eleven-year-old Margaret Jonas was at the arm's-length-yet-dreaming age. That is, in the light of day she kept all boys at an arm's length, just beyond touching range. But at night, she was just liable to dream about holding hands or even feeling their arm around her shoulder. Kissing, commonly referred to by adolescents as first base, was just beyond the boundaries of her budding imagination.

However, she was not interested in leaving every act motivated by her youthful curiosity in the realm of imagination. If her brother was friends with this Jewish boy, she wanted to meet him too. To accomplish that goal, all she had to do was walk the extremely short distance from her house—the Jonas house—to the cabin which she knew was his. She figured that he had to be there sometime before breakfast. She knew approximately what time that was, as she could always smell the toasted bread and the sulphur from the powdered scrambled eggs. The rising sun was just above ground level as she passed the *chadar ha-o-chel* and headed for the boys' cabins. The scent of breakfast abated. She passed a young girl, and then turned and caught her attention.

"Hey."

Sandy Singer turned around, her Jagger-Mills locks glistening in the thick early morning air. Margaret hesitated, realizing that she was a stranger in this strange and separate land of misplaced Israelites. Sandy responded with her Eastern accent, combined with an unexpected formality—even unexpected to her.

"Yes? May I help you?"

"Do you happen to know a…"

She was in too deep to withdraw now.

"um…"

"A who?"

"A…cute boy named Scott Malnick, by any chance?"

Why did she use that particular adjective? Sandy blinked slowly, and then her baby blue eyes widened. Her jealousy antennas perceived a possible interfering signal, even though she knew this girl was pre-pubescent, even behind Scotty.

"His *friends* call him Scotty."

"Oh. Right. I was wondering…where he might be right now."

"He'll be at breakfast."

"Oh. Do you think you could point him out?"

"You've never met him? I'll go one better. I'll introduce you to him."

"Oh, *no*. Just…point him out."

"Okay. Just curious. What cabin are you in? I don't think I've seen you around."

"I'm…I'm…just visiting."

"You have family at the camp?"

"Sort of."

Her father was no camper or camper's parent, but instead a laborer, the local help. She turned to leave. Just then, Sandy saw Scotty walking toward the *chadar ha-o-chel*. To Margaret's relief, Sandy said, "Well, anyway, there he is."

She pointed toward Scotty, who was meandering toward breakfast, chatting with Brandon Marks. Margaret blushed, and then remarked with an exhaling breath, "He is cute."

"He's a bit old for you, don't you think?"

"I know. Don't remind me."

Sandy chose to drop the subject. Anyway, they were about to enter the *chadar ha-o-chel*. Margaret walked away and toward her house without speaking a further word.

Breakfast on this summer morning consisted of French toast—definitely not from the culinary capital of the world—and home fries that looked more like *visiting* fries from Iceland, or some other cold country. Practically no one at Scotty's table besides Gus finished the whole thing, which provided Boris with some scraps for Bagel. Billy got sick and ended up throwing up in the semi-privacy of the bathroom situated at the end of the hall. If anyone sitting near it heard the retching sound, no one said anything.

Hebrew class with Geveret Brombeck was next. Scotty seriously considered performing his well-executed disappearing act. However, the watchful eye of Shlomo, who was walking right next to him like a watchful prison guard, interfered with his best laid plans. So, he prepared to endure another boring Hebrew lesson. These lessons always resulted in frustration over the ever-increasing number of unmemorized words, which, like snow during the opposite season, tended to pile up until the word *conversational* became an oxymoron.

Today's lesson, however, caught Scotty's attention instantly. Brombeck teased the assembled budding *talmidim*.

"Okay, young female Hebrew scholars, what does this romantic sentence mean?

"Anee o-hevet oat-cha."

There are always, on these occasions, a few "smart students" who know more going into the summer classes than most know coming out of them. They would know that the sentence is spoken from the girl's perspective. Sandy immediately spoke without being called on.

"I love you."

Did Scotty just see Sandy glance his way fleetingly, so subtly that it was akin to a strategic military signal?

"And the boy says…"

She continued.

"Anee o-hev oat-ach. That's I love you from a boy to a girl."

She sealed the signal with a fleeting smile. Scotty melted inside, as if a brand-new cutting-edge laser was burning a pinhole in his heart. Before this, he was conveniently infatuated. Now he was madly in love. He knew the unwritten Camp Chalutzim rules of the game, handed down like tribal mores from one summer to the next. Campers must move on to another momentary romance or abstain for the rest of the summer, like the celibate Shakers of Kentucky. But Scotty wasn't about to release the one thing that made this miserable summer bearable. He planned to practice a form of full summer monogamy with the only girlfriend he'd ever known. Now that she had professed her love anew for him in a carefully coded smile, he was hooked.

Chapter Twenty-Two

Stan Malnick was in the process of consuming two thirds of a small cheese pizza from Pizza Heaven when the turquoise kitchen wall phone rang above his head. His wife Doris, who was working on the other third, reached over and picked up the receiver.

"Hello, Rabbi."

Her expression clearly revealed maternal anxiety, if not outright fear. Stan was slow to perceive his wife's instant concern. On the other end of the line, Rabbi Menachem sat at his cluttered desk. He leaned back in his rolling chair to destress himself in the moment. Then he leaned forward with increased nervousness.

"No, everything is fine. Scotty is fine. He seems to be enjoying himself. No. No. It's all fine. Can I speak with Stan?"

She covered the phone.

"It's Rabbi Malmud."

Stan took the phone out of her hand and stood against the wall. Malmud continued.

"I just wanted to inform you and some of the other parents that we had a bit of a problem with one of the neighbors. But it's resolved."

"What kind of a problem?"

"Well...like I said, it's resolved. But just in case you happen to hear anything..."

"What happened?"

"Nothing, fortunately. But a next-door neighbor was engaging in perfectly legal target practice, although at night. We asked him to restrict any shooting..."

Stan stiffened.

"With a gun?"

"With a rifle. It was a rifle—a hunting rifle."

"What's the difference? That's what killed the president just nine months ago!"

"I know. But please, let me continue. The second amendment..."

Stan's face reddened.

"Don't talk politics with me. No crazy maniac is going to fire weapons anywhere near my son! We didn't pay more money than it was worth just to endanger my boy."

Rabbi Malmud sat up in his dark tan leather executive chair. He tried to deflect Malnick's anger with the proverbial soft answer that turns away wrath.

"Stan, the Torah tells us that it is Israel's divine Law, a lamp unto their feet and light unto their path. But it also tells us to obey the laws of the countries where we as Jews reside, outside the land of our ancestors. And the laws in this land allow hunting rifles to be used within certain guidelines. Apparently, Mr. Jonas is adhering to those guidelines."

"Don't patronize me with your professional rabbinical jargon, Malmud! I don't care *what* Torah tells us. You tell him...whoever it is... to fire his guns someplace else!"

"His name is Jonas...Robert Jonas."

"I don't care if his name is The Lone Ranger! Tell him to stay away from Camp Chalutzim!"

With a bang almost as loud as the shotgun at issue, Malnick slammed the receiver down. Doris spoke for the first time since she handed the phone to him.

"It's not good for your blood pressure or your heart, Stan. It's not worth it. And if Scotty knew we were arguing with the camp director like this..."

Stan shut his eyes and blew out an expiating breath. After a silent pause, he nodded—first a yes nod, and then a no nod, as if two contrary individuals were occupying his body at the same time. His face returned to its natural color, and then went beyond that to a pasty paleness not typical for summer.

"I'm not feeling well."

He left the room and headed for the hall and the grey carpeted steps to the second floor.

Chapter Twenty-Three

Rabbi Malmud had his favorite mitzvot, and mitzvot he left to others more adventurous than he was. Of all his mitzvot—and he was known to perform many larger and smaller good deeds—he called the one he derived most satisfaction from "Hidden Poverty." He created the term more than coined it. Coining implies a monetary transaction, and no coins were exchanged for services, as is the case with all mitzvot.

Malmud only practiced Hidden Poverty in the summer. During the rest of the year, he lived in a quiet suburban neighborhood, not far from the offices of the Jewish Community Relations Council, where he oversaw community outreach programs. There, he endeavored to present Jewish community concerns to the wider world. He joined forces with that world to oppose racism and antisemitism. Injustice lurked there, hidden or not. But this kind of poverty didn't exist there, or in the run-down inner city. It did, however, thrive *here*, mostly in rural areas, where the houses seemed statelier than in urban slums. But rotting wood showed through old paint like a wound under a scab.

After a short ride in a rickety yellow school bus, Shlomo and Lilly each engaged in pairing off campers from their respective cabins. Some of the selections ended up being natural, and some were chosen after the natural choices were formed. That wasn't what any of the counselors wanted, but coordination was lacking. Menachem Malmud was still reeling from stress related to Stan Malnick's angry accusation about the proximity of Robert Jonas' loaded rifle to Camp Chalutzim. So, he allowed things to evolve through a kind of natural selection. The result was somewhat unpredictable.

Sandy ended up with a mousy small girl named Fern, who had stringy red hair that always seemed in need of washing, even after a thorough shampooing. Fern had freckles that she detested. She thought she might be paired with Bunny. She realized they might look like a female Jewish Laurel and Hardy. But at least there would be little danger of a comparison between her and the attractive Mick Jagger-Hayley Mills combination that was cute-if-not-stunning Sandy Singer.

Scotty Malnick and Brandon Marks ended up together. That worked out well at first. Brandon knocked. A widow who must have been at least eighty years old took at least two minutes to come to the door. Scotty and Brandon were about to leave when they heard the tumbler click and turn several times. She shouted through the closed door in a wavering staccato cry.

"Yes? Who is it? What is it you want?"

Brandon shouted back.

"We're from Camp Chalutzim. We've come to help with anything you…you need, in the way of repair, or…"

"Oh. Oh, yes. They told me you were coming. Um…just a minute. Yes, I think I do have something. A banister that needs a bit of tightening… yes. Do you have a letter you can show me?"

They had been given a piece of paper signed by Rabbi Malmud. She opened the door a crack, as far as the chain would allow. They passed the letter to her. She pulled it in and read the few words of introduction.

"Yes, very good. This looks very good."

She opened the door wide. She was maybe five feet tall. Her grey hair was pulled back in a bun, her white glasses winged upward, and she wore a plain grey skirt that almost reached her ankles. But her plain white blouse was short sleeved, fitting for the hot summer.

"Well now. How nice of you two nice boys to come. Yes, you're from the camp. The Jewish one. First, let me give you this. It tells about the Savior. He was Jewish, you know. Oh yes, He was. Many people don't realize that. He was the greatest Jew who ever lived. He *was*."

Scotty took a small glossy tract from her. It was black and white, with a graphic design consisting of several question marks of various sizes. He hesitated, and then, as if it was too hot to handle, passed it to Brandon. Brandon in turn glanced at it and stuffed it in the pocket of his shorts. The woman smiled and nodded.

"You look like good boys. That tract will tell you how you can become Christians and know you're going to Heaven."

Finally, she let the boys in. Scotty's eyes were immediately "stared down" by the eyes of a familiar depiction hanging on the stairwell wall. There, perhaps eight or nine feet away, was the well-known American Christian painting of Jesus, from the robed shoulder up, letting the welcome visitor know just who it was that the woman worshipped in this humble home. Brandon chose not to tell the lady that he believed in the One she was endeavoring to recommend. He was sure that would make Scotty uncomfortable.

"Well, here's the banister."

She put her hand on the fixture needing repair. Then she shook it for emphasis, while she put her other hand on her cheek. It jiggled like the loose handlebars on his back-home outgrown and long-since-junked bicycle.

"Oh, silly me. Let me go get the screwdriver."

She raised her finger like a "schoolmarm" in the inimitable prairie.

"I'll be back in a flash."

She took a bit longer than that. When she returned, she had the promised screwdriver in her hand. Scotty realized that she probably could have tightened the screws herself. But he figured that she was a widow, and so wouldn't think of it. He had no evidence for that conclusion, but he was nevertheless convinced of it. She gave the tool to Brandon, and he tightened the screws. That being accomplished, it was time to move on.

Somehow, Scotty and Brandon never mentioned their names, and the woman never mentioned her name. But their next experience was different, as they ended up at the Jonas house. Scotty worked up the courage before knocking on the door. It was his turn. He had no idea that he was standing at the entrance to the house where his new-found friend Mack lived, where Lilly had recently visited. He hesitated. Then he reached over and tapped the door three quick times. There was no response, and, relieved, he turned to leave. Unconscious stress eased and the tense muscles at the back of his neck momentarily slackened. His baby-like features and short stature made all these introductions and offers more intimidating for him. Just then, the door struggled to free itself from the tumbling lock, and then swung open. Scotty had no choice but to pivot back.

Tricia Jonas stood in the doorway. Her blonde hair was pulled back by a now bright blue band. Scotty could see the rifle, which was perched in a rack on the mantle. Then his eyes crossed a series of framed pictures, lined up in three rows. Even though the age of the boy in the frame was much younger than he and Scotty were now, he clearly identified Mack. In the kind of extraordinary flash response that bypasses reason, Scotty stepped back. He instantly wanted to walk away from the extreme awkwardness of the moment, his identity as Mack's friend remaining as hidden as the poverty that he was told lurked throughout the neighborhood. Tricia was about to suggest some ideas, based on her memory of the "Hidden Poverty" day in other years. After all, Robert was out of the house, and so an opportunity to help presented itself. But Scotty was in a hurry to leave. Tricia smiled.

"Hi. I'm Tricia Jonas. And who are you two boys?"

Without any explanation to Brandon, Scotty lamely excused himself.

"Um…sorry. I've got to go. I mean, we've got to go…to go back…I mean, we can't help…right now."

Brandon was clearly confused.

"We can't?"

Scotty took his arm and pulled him away. He turned, and then began his retreat.

"Right. Bye."

Tricia shut the door, or perhaps it was more of a slam. Brandon shook off Scotty's arm.

"What are you doing?"

"I'll explain later…maybe. There are plenty of other hidden poverty houses. Can't you see them?"

"You're crazy."

"Yes, I suppose I am."

Chapter Twenty-Four

Late that night, several mosquitos orbited the lone naked light source beyond the screened window, whizzing around the incandescent globe like astronaut John Glenn. Scotty tried counting them, but they were a poor substitute for sheep. He lay there on his back, still and wrapped in his stiff sheets and thin scratchy cover. He had no way of knowing exactly how much time had passed. He intentionally closed his eyes, wanting the night to be over, even though he had nothing to look forward to the next day except a breakfast of papery eggs and acidic orange juice. Sure enough, the strategy worked, and he drifted into a light sleep—and yet not so light that he didn't dream.

Scotty's dream was the kind that registers in the unconscious before dissolving with the dawn. But it leaves the fading shadow of the ethereal and often irrational kingdom that was temporarily erected. In that alternative world, Scotty had grown tall—very tall. He didn't change in the normal ways—pubic hair, a beard, or a five o'clock shadow. He was just *tall*, towering over Brandon, Gus, Sandy, Billy—even his parents, who had been transported through the miracle of a dream state, and who had their own cots in Billy's cabin. Scotty was taller than all of them; smooth skinned, with a boyish face, but tall, towering over them all.

Then suddenly, the world around Scotty became noisy. There was a throaty cough that surprised Scotty, noise from all corners of the room. And then he was up, his sleep state torn from him like a cold slap. He sat up in his cot. Billy was outside Scotty's cabin, several yards from the screened window. Every boy in the cabin was awake now, attracted to the origin of the painful retching. They vied with each other to get the best view as they peered out the window. There in the light of the bare bulb, on his knees next to Billy, was Shlomo. Billy was now doubled over and lying on his side. Shlomo handed him some paper towels and placed a wet cloth towel on his forehead. A distant faint siren swelled louder and louder, until it was so loud that it ricocheted off the windowpanes and iron cot frames. A fire-engine red ambulance sped up the gravel road from the camp entrance and screeched to a halt not far from Scotty's cabin. Two men walked over to Billy. Within the space of a minute, they had him on a stretcher. He was obviously in pain. A few seconds later they sped away, sirens blaring and tires spinning.

Scotty couldn't say exactly how he knew that Billy Bitner would be back. Perhaps it was the fight in his eyes, the stubborn will to be normal, the hunger to be with boys doing boy things, like baseball. After all, he wasn't a bad batter. And he could catch a line drive almost as well as Shlomo, who was himself impressive—that is, for a Camp Chalutzim counselor.

But for now, the show was over. No one had to persuade the campers to go back to bed. The darkness had its own way of communicating that message. Everyone was under their covers within a few minutes. Scotty's eyes scanned the cots. He noticed that one was shaped like a tent with a human pole. That cot, of course, belonged to Brandon Marks. His flashlight couldn't penetrate both sheet and blanket, so it acted as an opaque shield against any curious parties. That was necessary, since the secret book was no longer a secret. But this was the middle of the night, and everyone except Scotty and Brandon was asleep or on their way to dreamland. Scotty knew he wouldn't be able to follow suit. At least he could use the bathroom in privacy, although he had no urge presently. He gingerly moved his covers aside and swung around until he sat up on the side of his cot. Then he got up and went over to Brandon's "tent." He tapped lightly on the "tent pole" that was Brandon's shoulder. That startled him, and he threw off the sheet. The flashlight swung up and its beam crossed the wooden rafters, until it shined through the window like a distress beacon.

"What is it you want, Malnick?"

"Shh…"

"What is it? Can't you see I'm reading?" Brandon whispered loudly.

"Don't you ever read anything but that book?" Scotty practically mouthed, endeavoring to keep the conversation as private as possible.

"Of course I do. What kind of a question is that?"

"I just mean you read that a lot."

"So? Benny reads the siddur all the time."

"Yeah, but he *has* to. I mean, he davens and everything. It's how he prays. He doesn't just read to read, like you'd read a book, like you'd read *The Catcher in the Rye*, or *Dr. No*."

"Right. Well, it's like this. Every time I read something I've read before, I see something new. That's how the Bible is different."

"You mean like the Jewish Bible?"

"It's all the Jewish Bible."

"No, it isn't. There's the Jewish Bible, and the other Bible. *Their* Bible."

"It's *all* Jewish."

"Oh, come on. There's our Bible, I mean my Bible, and then there's their Bible."

"If you say so. You haven't even read what's in my Bible, so how would you know what's in it?"

Scotty couldn't tell Brandon that he had peeked at Brandon's New

Testament. And he in no way would let him know that he was surprised by what he read in that Matthew part. He responded with words he'd heard in afternoon Hebrew School.

"Jews don't read the New Testament."

"Lilly has."

"Well…just forget it."

And that's just what happened—that is, as a figure of speech. The reality was, of course, a different matter. The conversation would not be forgotten. In fact, it would be remembered whenever Scotty thought about Brandon for even a millisecond.

Chapter Twenty-Five

As the summer crawled beyond solstice like a caterpillar whose butterfly prospects were suspect, crushes—or the fleeting shadow of them—passed over one camper couple after another. Sometimes the shadows were so fleeting that the results seemed almost like an innocent form of polygamy. Crushes collided with one another like ships crashing in the night, but without any damage. These were, after all, still shadows.

Some of the matches could hardly be called that. Gus' squarish haircut appeared more like a circle next to Fern's slight skinny "numeral one" figure. Her body was waif-thin and fragile in appearance. Together, they added up to a cardinal ten, and they quickly became the latest Camp Chalutzim item across all ages. When they held clammy hands, everyone tried not to stare. The truth was, Gus didn't know what to do with this odd relationship. He was embarrassed about the whole thing. Fern pressured him into "going" with her, and indeed she had a good reason for doing so. Almost as soon as the "contract" was informally sealed—indeed the next morning over a hot-off-the-press pancake breakfast—Fern released the news to every table adjacent to where she was seated. She was going with Gus Simmons! She spoke those words with energy she tried and failed to conceal. But she had no words for the feeling of intense insecurity that she was experiencing. Nevertheless, it drove every elevated word. Gus was Scotty's only friend that summer—that is, among the campers at Camp Chalutzim. He slept in a bunk just a few feet from him. And now his entire focus would be directed toward the skinny girl with stringy red hair. She was no Sandy Singer. But in this "square dance" world of changing partners, every boy was bound to be paired with every girl sooner or later, depending on the remaining days left.

Scotty sat at breakfast quietly consuming pancakes and artificial maple syrup. No one could see his aching heart under his Chalutzim tee shirt. Mack Jonas turned out to be a good friend, but he lived outside that insular world. Scotty figured he could wait out the expected short period of time until the tryst between Gus and Fern ran out of thin mountain oxygen. He could pass the time at the *Fortress of Solitude*, with or without man's best friend Bagel. And then he'd have Gus to hang out with again.

However, the expected partner-changing never occurred. Fern didn't turn out to be what Gus expected—a short summer flame which flickers and dies in a few days. That evening as darkness began to descend and the usual Camp Chalutzim protocol of holding hands commenced, he experienced something he'd never felt before in his short life. Fern's thin hand was vulnerable and delicate in his thick and enfolding hand. As they walked in the usual "paired off" silence, he suddenly stopped short, pulling her to a stop with him. He turned and faced her. She reddened and her eyes moistened as tears began to stream down her face.

"What did I do wrong? Did I do something wrong? Please…please don't tell the boys I'm ugly. I…I wish…I…wasn't here at this…this…camp. I wish…I wish…I hate it!"

"Ugly? Ugly?"

He paused, and then repeated the question.

"Ugly? Are you kidding me?"

She began to tremble as the tears ran down her cheeks. He let go of her hand, and she tried to wipe her tears with her left hand.

"Are you kidding me?"

He looked into her glassy green eyes. She trembled.

"What? What did I do wrong? Tell me. What? I know I'm no...no Sandy."

"Ugly?" he repeated.

"I mean, compared to Sandy, I know I'm ugly. *Everybody* knows it."

"Stop!"

"What? What?"

"Yes, Sandy's *cute*."

Fern rolled her eyes.

"Don't remind me."

"Yeah, but you...*you're* beautiful. And your big green eyes caught my attention on the first day of camp."

"I don't believe you. You're telling me that now. And then when you're with the other boys, well...you know..."

"I know what?"

"*You* know. *You know*."

She looked down at her off-white sneakers as she spoke barely above a whisper.

"Well, tomorrow morning, we'll both move on. I understand."

After an awkward pause, Gus whispered back, "Well, we'll *all* move on when camp is over. But not tomorrow. And not the next day. And the truth is, I enjoy talking to you, and spending time with you. *That's* the truth."

Fern smiled and squeezed his hand.

"You're sweet. I hope we both come back next year."

"I never thought I'd say this, but I actually hope I come back... especially if you're here."

He took her hand, and they walked the rest of the way to the cabins.

Chapter Twenty-Six

The next day, July 18, was a Saturday. Scotty's summer had been a combination of daily mundane routines and periodic surprises. This day was one of those "surprise" days. He knew there would be no recorded crackly trumpet reveille. That was expected for Shabbat. The tradition of abstaining from musical instruments was a given, although it never made much sense to him. After all, quiet music calmed him down. Wasn't that a form of resting? And records negated the need for live playing. However, records were electrically reproduced, and Scotty had been informed that turning on an electrical switch was akin to lighting a fire, and forbidden on the Shabbat. So, recordings too were a no-go.

The usual breakfast of papery eggs and puffy rolls was usually followed by the expected Shabbat service. And that was true on this day as well. Everyone assembled in the *bay-dam ha-gadol*, and the usual chanting ensued. However, in the middle of the service, everyone arose, as if on cue. This was one of those surprises. He followed a line of campers out of the hall and onto the grounds. He turned to Orthodox Benny. Maybe he could tell him what was going on and let him in on the camp-wide secret.

"What's happening? Is it some kind of fire alarm without the alarm?"

"No, dummy. It's Tisha B'Av, the ninth of Av."

"Oh."

No one clued him in on the tradition that day. It was only after Shlomo mentioned it later that he understood it was an act of mourning over the destruction of two—that's right, two—temples way back there somewhere in the foggy Jewish past. Scotty knew about the Holocaust. His father would never let him forget. But this one was a new one on him.

Shlomo read from the Bible—the Book of Lamentations, to be exact—while they marched hypnotically, like the Eloi in the 1960 film "The Time Machine" which he and a few friends had seen at a Saturday matinee during a much more enjoyable summer the year before.

Just when Scotty thought the surprises were over for the day, Billy, who was marching aimlessly two boys ahead of him, collapsed like a spindly chair. Having never seen anyone just fold under himself like that, Scotty was shocked. Shlomo and Lilly instantly jumped to Billy's aid. Shlomo called out the first reliable name he could think of. As controversial as Brandon Marks' book had become, Shlomo perhaps unconsciously thought Brandon's controversial convictions might make him reliable— like a member of Philadelphia's cult leader Father Divine, who ensured moral behavior in his adherents.

"Brandon! Brandon Marks! Bo Hey'na! Come here! Run like the wind to Rabbi Malmud's office and tell him or whoever's there to call an ambulance for Billy. Hurry! Tell him we're on the path to the *bay-dam ha-gadol*. Now!"

With Brandon gone, Scotty allowed his racing thoughts to catch up with him.

Oh no. What'll happen? What'll happen to Billy? What if... and then what...what of Billy? What if he's not. What will be left of him? What if he's gone to...to nowhere...or somewhere. I don't know.

Then he lifted his eyes towards the heavens.

"If you're out there…whoever you are, don't let Billy…"

Then he reverted to self-talk.

"I mean, I hope Billy will be okay. I hope so."

If someone was out there…if. Billy *had* to be okay. He wasn't allowed to die in summer camp. Not at Camp Chalutzim. That would *really* be something to mourn about. Scotty could hear sirens sounding, louder and louder, crying out like the Greek sirens of ancient myth, wooing Billy towards his destiny, toward his…No! He *had* to live.

Scotty didn't know anyone who had died in his family, even his grandparents. His parents' generation knew many family members who died in the Holocaust. And that catastrophe was one reason for the Tisha B'Av march. But it *couldn't* happen here, at Camp Chalutzim. It *couldn't*.

The same two ambulance drivers that picked up Billy before repeated their task. If they were concerned for Billy, they didn't express it. They just performed their duties faithfully. This was years before emergency personnel were trained in emergency resuscitation efforts. So they acted as conveyors to the emergency room where others would take over. They proceeded to remove the stretcher from the rear of the vehicle; methodically, mechanically. Brandon was back by this time, and he had a look on his face that Scotty hadn't seen before.

Brandon too was trying to pray. He had seen more answers to prayer than any of the other boys had. And yet, the heavens seemed like brass to him.

By that evening, a stifling spiritual stench of death overhung the warm and humid fields of Camp Chalutzim, not unlike the oppressive suffocation surrounding the previous November all throughout the world.

By that night, the Tisha B'Av memorial march of death had transitioned to a pre-taps recitation of the ancient Kaddish, marking Billy's death. It was spoken by a grieving Rabbi Malmud. Billy hadn't just disappeared from his vacant cabin cot. He had disappeared from this present life, never to return. For the campers left behind, there would be no funeral to attend, and no opportunity to process the finality together. No one at Camp Chalutzim knew exactly when a funeral would be held.

After the short public address liturgical service, the long day dedicated to death—the two ancient Temples, the Crusades, the Inquisition, the pogroms, the Holocaust victims—and finally, Billy—ended. Scotty was left to wonder, as he stared at the mosquitos orbiting the lamp just beyond the screen window, what this existence was all about—and what an eternity of blank and vacuous nothingness like the one he was convinced Billy had embarked on could possibly be like. But what about that Voice? And what about Brandon's book, and the One it spoke of?

Chapter Twenty-Seven

Unknown to the campers—and even the counselors—Rabbi Malmud called for a meeting with his full office staff of three, to be held after breakfast the next morning. He entrusted small invitational slips of paper to Efraim, a reliable senior in his last summer at Camp Chalutzim. His fringes—or tzitzit—practically flying in the wind as his thin frame wended its way between campers and tables, he distributed the slips to the three office staff workers.

After breakfast, the small staff retreated to Malmud's office and sat in front of his cluttered desk. He hadn't slept, and the exhaustion was clearly visible beneath his eyes, like President Kennedy during his last year in office. He looked down, then up, then stared at the space between the staff before him.

"Um…just between us…I just want to say…that…"

His weariness bled through his words and sighs.

"That…I considered canceling the rest of the summer…"

There was an audible gasp from more than one of his staff.

"But…that would be too complicated."

As soon as he spoke those words, he regretted saying them. He had planned to smother any emotional evidence of the depression he was feeling in the aftermath of Billy's Tisha B'Av death, and the attendant guilt over whether he could have prevented it by insisting that Billy not come to camp—or at least be sent home at the first hint of any symptoms which he, as the director, should have been on the lookout for.

The staff didn't respond well to Menachem Malmud's admission. It clearly had a demoralizing effect. With no need for electronic bugging, the word leaked out that the rest of the camp year might be canceled, despite the understanding that no discussion in the director's office was to travel beyond its supposedly secure doors. No one admitted to the infraction. Perhaps every ear in the office was guilty of the leak. Wherever the guilt lay, the news spread like the *Angel of Death* mist in DeMille's 1956 epic *The Ten Commandments*. By early evening, it had spread to every table in the *chadar ha-o-chel*. At first, no one felt free to bring it up. But Gus Simmons shared it with Scotty amidst the usual dinner din. Scotty secretly hoped it was true, but he didn't really believe it. Consequently, he didn't pass it on. But as is typical of leaks, it traveled to the girls' table and ended up tickling Fern's ears, who had heard it from Sandy. That's all it took to permeate the entire hall, like forbidden yeast during Passover.

By nightfall, it seemed as if every counselor throughout the camp was trying to reassure their campers that no one was going anywhere. And by morning, the crisis had died down. Scotty experienced a letdown that stirred up a new case of homesickness. And Shlomo's Columbia Records grey seal copy of "My Fair Lady" that Shlomo played that evening didn't help. It only served to remind Scotty of the street where he lived. This was closely followed by the melancholy strains of Taps, which was once again followed by the planetary circuit of the mosquitos. And this in turn was followed by the subterranean flashlight under Brandon Marks' covers. He was once again reading the only book he ever seemed to read. And Scotty was left with the few words he could remember. "Let your light so shine." Brandon's flashlight soon clicked off, and Scotty turned over and drifted off into a vivid dream.

In Scotty's dream, camp didn't look like camp. There was a hill, high and grassy, and some barnyard animals dotted here and there. Mostly there were lambs like the ones he had seen in movies, TV shows, the petting zoo, and books. He reached out and petted one. It felt more like his scratchy wool blanket than a sheep's coat. It turned and looked at him, betraying as much of a smile as a lamb might be capable of. He waited for it to speak, but even in his dream, he knew that lambs aren't capable of human speech—only a baa here and there. Then he noticed that the young animal wasn't so much looking at him as it was looking just past him, or rather beyond him. Curious, his dream-self turned to see what the lamb saw. As he turned, he sensed an increasing glow, as if the light was operated by a rheostat. At 180 degrees, the light was so bright he found himself squinting. A tall figure in an electric whiter-than-white garment stood in front of him. Then, in a whisper befitting the time of night and everyone else's dream state, the gentlest voice he had ever heard spoke.

"Scott, let *YOUR* light shine."

Very few people called him Scott. He was always Scotty. However, his father did. He always called him Scott. He was surprised to hear *this* voice call him that. After all, this obviously wasn't his father. But he was more surprised to hear that quote that he'd read so recently under the covers and heard in Lilly's folk song. And he was likewise surprised by the way it was quoted. He quickly realized that this was supposed to be Jesus, or someone playing Jesus, like Jeffrey Hunter in 1960's *King of Kings*. That film was part of the spate of Biblical epics that began in the early fifties. He had seen it with his family.

"Scott, let *YOUR* light shine," the voice repeated emphatically. And then, like Hamlet's father, the apparition, or whatever it was, left.

Chapter Twenty-Eight

When Scotty first woke up, the dream remained for a few seconds, like the closed-eyes afterimage of the sun. Then it began to fade into the irretrievable archive of Scotty's prior dreams. What did remain was the infantile body attached to his technically adolescent mind. And then the shame returned, and with it the struggle to conceal the pre-pubescent evidence.

The day unfolded with the telltale creases of weekday after weekday before it. And *Z'man Chofshee* after lunch was likewise typical, with one difference. As he began to select plantain weeds in the *Fortress of Solitude*, he realized that the announcer in his head was absent. In its place was that gentle voice repeating the same words he had heard the night before—the words from Brandon's book. *Let your light shine.*

He returned to the cabin just in time to see Benny challenging Gus.

"What is it with you and Fern? Flattie freckled Fern. There are certainly better-looking fish in the sea, Gus. Don't you think you should have moved on by now?"

With the weight of rabbinic authority on his side, Benny admonished him further.

"You shouldn't be touching her during her niddah, and you don't know when that is."

"Leave me alone, Kahn. She probably doesn't even have her period yet."

"You don't know that, Simmons."

"Go haunt someone else, Benny. There are plenty of girls who are mature enough to knock your block off."

From across the room, a lone voice tried to encourage Gus, although the camper ended up falling short.

"You must admit she's kind of ugly, Gus. Maybe you should move on."

That triggered first a few giggles and then a mounting consensus, ending with a chant that ended with applause.

"Dump her, dump her, dump her! She's ugly, ugly, ugly!"

All the pressure wore Gus down, and he acquiesced to the lie.

"I'll think about it. Just stop bugging me."

Just then, Shlomo entered the cabin. All talk about Fern ceased. At first, Gus experienced relief. Like skipping a track on one of Shlomo's Broadway albums, the banter turned to the latest New York Yankees and St. Louis Cardinals conquests. Then, the scent of baking dinner rolls reached his olfactory center. With all the conflict, he had considered skipping dinner, but the rolls called to him like the wispy whiff of aroma beckoning a starving cartoon character to float on air.

When Gus finally arrived at the *chadar ha-o-chel* for a meat meal of hamburgers and iceberg lettuce salads, he finally made up his mind to move on from Fern, even though it meant breaking his word to her. He walked past her table, and then continued to ignore her in favor of his rusty lettuce and flat-as-his-mattress burger. As the meal progressed, Fern became more and more agitated. She wanted to stare at Gus, but she was behind him, and he was concentrating on his dinner. Finally, she got up and walked out of the *chadar ha-o-chel* and into the approaching dusk. She teared up, wishing the impending darkness would enfold and obscure her. She hoped no one would notice she was gone. But someone had. Brandon Marks had finished eating and was headed to the *Fortress of Solitude* for a few quiet minutes of reflection, if not out and out prayer. He caught a quick glance of Fern's flushed face and stopped short. He hoped she hadn't seen him, as she had hoped the same. He turned on his heels and then froze. But that only made him more conspicuous, as if he was posing for a portrait right there on the path. Fern crowed at him, putting her hands on her hips like Peter Pan.

"Look at you! Running from something, Brandon? Tell your buddy Gus he's a liar and a fake. And friends like you are too!"

Then she stomped away, leaving him standing there feeling accused, swept up, implicated in affairs he had no control over. He felt that strange guilt that accompanies association, like Joe McCarthy's "have you now or have you ever been associated with" accusation from ten years earlier. When everyone had moved on, he finally did as well—to the *Fortress of Solitude.*

Chapter Twenty-Nine

With a few weeks of camp left, the Jonas house was quiet. Tricia was washing the dinner dishes, hoping vainly that Robert had forgotten what night it was. He never did, except once. On that occasion, a sprained foot distracted him from his weekly habit. But he was healthy now... healthy and ready. He searched the kitchen.

"Where's my cap?"

"Wherever you left it," she responded dryly.

"Okay. Okay. I think I left it in the car."

"It's not in the car. I would have noticed it. I drove Margaret and her friends to Barb's house where she's staying overnight tonight. Did you check the bedroom? I mean, it's bright purple with those huge letters. 'Purple Patriots.' How could you ever miss that ridiculous thing?"

Robert stomped up to the bedroom. Tricia could hear him rummaging around.

"Don't you dare make a mess up there!"

He almost jumped down the stairs, with the prized hat on his head. Margaret stood at the kitchen sink with her back to him as he opened the front door. When she was in the single digits, she pleaded with her father to take her to the weekly meetings with him. He would stoop down to her level and explain to her that she was too young, and that someday she would come with Tricia and him, when she understood more about her heritage as a Christian American. Now that she was eleven, she understood more about that combined subject than she wanted to know, and she had no interest in the Purple Patriots and their weekly Tuesday night meetings. She was much more interested in a particular person who would be excluded from those gatherings—namely adorably cute Scotty Malnick. And although Robert was concerned for Mack and Margaret's education in these matters, the weekly meetings were at this point restricted to male adults. That was okay with him—for now.

Traffic was snarled on the highway. Robert could see the emergency vehicle lights blinking red and white in the distance. And he could hear the sirens of more vehicles racing to the scene. A few cars were endeavoring to navigate the berm. But those were becoming just a part of the clogged arteries that threatened to give every frustrated driver a heart attack—figuratively.

When Robert finally arrived at the small, rented hall where the meetings were held, he was a half hour late and breathing hard. Everyone had some sort of document in their hands. Faithful member Ralph Messer stood over him and whispered.

"You're late."

"Just gimme the sheets."

Every week, another member of the group officiated, reflecting the American democratic spirit behind the meetings—what *they* saw as the American democratic spirit. That is, every participant was a white Protestant. That week it was Richard Starks.

"You have before you your homework for next week. At that time, we will discuss this important document, which has been endorsed by none other than the self-made patriotic industrialist Henry Ford—in whose wonderful automobiles some of you drove to this very meeting. He published this article in his Dearborn Michigan newspaper before the war. Therefore, everything in it must be true."

Robert read the title at the top of the sheet. *The Protocols of the Elders of Zion: Abridged.* Then Starks gave the Cliff notes of the abridged version.

A small group of Jews control the world. Our nation is at risk. We must spread the word.

Robert clutched the sheets. He knew he had to be a soldier in this army. And he had to begin at home.

Chapter Thirty

The Jonas house was dark by the time Robert pulled into the driveway in his 1960 olive green Ford Falcon. He bought it new, and it was almost paid off. Just one year to go. Henry Ford himself would be proud of the Purple Patriots meeting, he mused. He entered the house and placed the keys in a cut glass candy dish by the door. He had long ago made that a habit so he wouldn't misplace them.

Everyone was asleep. But Robert was too stirred up by the meeting to go to bed. He wanted to tell especially Mack and Margaret about *The Protocols*. He knew he wouldn't be able to sleep until the Jonas walls reverberated with the truth he carried like Paul Revere on his midnight ride—even if no eardrums followed suit. So, he spoke as if every kitchen chair was occupied, and a few Purple Patriots were crowded along the walls SRO. The vacuous room stared back at him. But that didn't faze him. His voice rose and fell melodically, as befit the occasion.

"We are in grave danger, family. I'm speaking to you, Mack. I'm speaking to you, Margaret. Yes, *you*. Beware of the danger lurking right next door. Yes, right outside our windows."

He paused. Something was wrong. That was the wrong approach.

"It sounds too much like Harold Hill hawking his wares in 'The

Music Man," he mumbled to himself. He had seen the 1962 film version, and he had no interest in flimflammery. He began again.

"I just came back from my weekly meeting. I want you all to read this, and then we'll talk about it."

That was better. He stretched out his hand with the sheets in it. He knew that he hadn't read it. But that was beside the point. He knew all he needed to know about what it said. Now Tricia needed to know. Mack needed to know. Margaret needed to know.

He was so excited about educating his family on the insidious plans afoot that he overslept and arrived in the kitchen amidst a typical rushed Pop Tart breakfast. The pastry was introduced the year before, in 1963, and the convenience novelty was at its zenith. Even on a summer morning, with typical household chores and workday responsibilities waiting, it produced a toaster-popping breakfast pace that left little room for Robert's lecture. He would have to wait for a more opportune time to share—and then for an even more perfect time in the increasingly tumultuous future to act.

Scotty was unaware of the ticking time bomb next door. He was instead consumed with numbers—that is, the number of days left in his Camp Chalutzim confinement. How many minutes, adding up to hours, would be dedicated to the artistry of his quick-change from t-shirt and shorts to striped pajamas? Although there was no place in the cabin for a wall calendar dedicated to a countdown, counting had become an obsession that occupied time spent in the *Fortress of Solitude* while he shot plantain weeds. The plantain world series had begun, and Scotty's A team was trouncing his B team. All the players were anxious for the season to end so they could go home—to the room, and the rug, and the inane afternoon Hanna-Barbera cartoons—to a time well wasted before the dreaded school year commenced.

Chapter Thirty-One

That night, Scotty couldn't sleep. He tried out various positions, but none of them availed. At three in the morning, which he could just make out on the moon-reflected dial belonging to Shlomo's collapsible shell clock, he was noon-hour wide awake. The red dye in dinner's bug juice acted as an unprescribed amphetamine. By the time he finally dozed off, it was six-thirty, and everyone was up. His exhaustion brought with it a clumsy fumbling ineptitude. Somewhere between shedding his pajamas and donning his underpants, there was a fleeting second of revelation—an unmistakable exposure that revealed the "naked" truth Scotty had been carefully concealing from everyone in the cabin. But that concealment ended when pink and pudgy Malcolm Berman, who had become a bit less pudgy and more physically mature in the last few weeks, pointed his finger at Scotty's presently vulnerable organ and blurted out, "Look at Malnick's baby wee-wee."

Scotty's face turned red as he grabbed a towel from his bureau and hurriedly wrapped it around him. He closed his eyes and tried desperately to keep tears from escaping, which proved impossible. Then, after he wiped his eyes with the back of his free hand, he finally went about the mundane business of dressing. Half the boys had already left for Shacharit service, and then for breakfast. Scotty walked out of the screen door and into an iron-grey morning. He had no intention of joining anyone doing anything, let alone going to services and breakfast. He had no appetite for either. He walked off unnoticed and headed for the camp entrance. He had no specific plan in his mind. He only wanted to leave this unpleasant place.

When he reached the Camp Chalutzim sign at the entrance, he paused, like a collared dog restrained by the shock of an invisible electric fence. Hesitantly, he summoned up the courage to walk through it. Once he did, he didn't experience liberation, which he had expected. And there was no electric shock. Instead, he sensed fear. He had broken out more than he had broken through. And he was sure to get caught. But he had come this far. Civilization lay in the distance. The ribbon of highway awaited him. On this two-lane road—with signs of the hidden poverty Shlomo referred to all around him—he could see an old gas station in the distance, and on the other side a *greasy spoon* of some sort, with a half working red neon light flashing above it blinking *Open, Open, Open*. But he had no change in his pocket to purchase anything. And anyway, he had a more important goal in mind—home.

He'd been walking for maybe a half hour when it finally occurred to him that he would never reach his warmly carpeted bedroom this way. He had never hitchhiked. That was for the older, more experienced teens, the kind that enjoyed playing hooky from school. But if he was to navigate the miles and miles and miles it took to arrive at home sweet home, he would have to travel by something faster than his Keds. He had been warned by both parents about the dangers of hitchhiking. His mother even related the story of a boy who was stabbed a dozen times by a wild-eyed teen driver, and left on the side of the road, only to be run over by another speeding driver. He doubted the veracity of the account, but it did achieve its effect at the time. He chose to ignore it now. He worked up the courage to tentatively stick his thumb out.

It didn't take thirty seconds for a gleaming new 1963 black Corvette Stingray to pull over just ahead of him. A window rolled down and a head stuck out, cigarette in mouth.

"Get your ass in here. I can take you as far as the highway, maybe thirty miles."

Scotty hadn't really expected things to develop this far. But this was the highway to home, and the car was headed the right direction. Still, he wished the driver were a bit more mature. But he couldn't say no now.

He walked back and waited for the shotgun passenger to get out and let him in the red leather back seat. There were two other boys back there. Once he was seated, the car took off, wheels skidding on the graveled berm as it gained traction. Right away, Scotty could sense that the name of the game was *scare the stranger*.

At seventy miles-per-hour on the straight road, the driver took his hands off the wheel. Scotty could see slower moving traffic in the distance. For the second time— the dire situation with Billy Bitner being the first— Scotty the agnostic prayed that he would live through this frightening situation. No sooner had he begun to move his silent lips than he heard a siren build to a crescendo. A police cruiser outgunning the Corvette pulled alongside them, its loudspeaker demanding, "Pull over!" The Corvette slowed down.

"Get out, all of you! Turn around and put your hands on the car. All right. Let me see your license. Where are you all from?"

The driver smirked as he handed his license over and turned around. The cop shook his head and muttered.

"Temporary. It figures. This isn't your first run-in, is it?"

After a pause he shouted, *"Is it?"*

Finally, the driver whispered, "No, sir."

The cop went back over to the cruiser and grabbed the police radio mic.

"Ralston, car one-two-eight."

A crackly voice responded with barely intelligible words. Then he responded, "Roger on that." Then the radio responded again with more barely intelligible words. The policeman turned to Scotty, realizing he wasn't from the area.

"Where are *you* from?"

"Um…the camp."

"The Jewish one?"

Scotty felt embarrassed about his Jewish identity, but he couldn't very well deny his religious status—at least in these parts.

"Well?"

"Yes, sir. Camp Chalutzim, sir."

"Well, what the hell are you doing out here?"

Scotty chose to remain silent, which would not become the law of the land until two years later. The policeman was about to insist that he explain himself, but then changed his mind and turned to his radio instead.

"I got a kid from the Jewish camp here on highway marker twenty-eight. Tell someone to come get him."

He turned to Scotty.

"Okay. Get in, kid."

For the next awkward ten minutes, Scotty sat in the back seat of the police cruiser, feeling like a felon. Finally, Boris pulled up in his 1955 Nash Rambler. He slammed the car door and walked briskly over to Scotty.

"What you doing here? Shlomo will be very mad. Yes, and Rabbi Malmud will be very mad also. No. He is *now* very mad! I hear him earlier shouting some not nice things. Maybe he will even send you home from this place."

Scotty could hear his own silent thoughts scream, *Good! Send me home.* The policeman, however, seemed impatient to get on with his day.

"Are we finished here?"

"Yes, we finish. I take him back to Camp Chalutzim."

"All right. You do that."

He turned to Scotty and pulled all the rank he could, knowing that he didn't have the authority he claimed. But he had made big claims before with truant children, to "scare" them into behaving, and that was the authoritarian voice he had used.

"If I see you out here again, I'll take you into juvenile detention and lock you up until your parents come and get you."

All Scotty could think as he got in Boris's car was, *it's better than the prison I've been at all summer.*

Chapter Thirty-Two

As the little Nash Rambler navigated between the right-hand lane and the passing lane at least ten miles over the speed limit, an exasperated Boris questioned Scotty.

"Why you run from camp?"

Scotty saw no need to answer anything. He sat stoically, facing forward with arms folded, and with a resistant expression Boris couldn't see. Not content with silence, Boris broke it again.

"Well?"

Scotty didn't want to tell this strange foreigner anything. But if he was going to share anything, he would burn his ears with his utter disdain for everything about this whole place and summer. It took one more prodding repetition for Scotty to lob a teenager's arsenal of rage.

"I hate this place. I hate my bunkmates, I hate my counselors, I hate the lousy food you cook, I hate the religious services, I hate *everything*!"

Boris paused as he considered his next words. Should he share things he considered so personal that he had never shared them with anyone in the West outside of his small community of "escapees"? As private as they were, he felt they might give some perspective to this clueless child. He decided to present an understanding tone.

"I tell you, I too went to camp I hated. So, I…I know."

"I didn't know they had summer camps there. What was it called?"

"It was called gulag. All year. Not pleasant. Terrible food, like Ivan the Terrible."

Scotty missed the humor. Boris continued.

"I was what they call refusenik. We did not have freedom like here. Yours is better camp. But I understand that you don't like it. That is okay. But there was one guard who liked me. I will tell you secret, but you tell no one. You promise."

Another pause.

"Okay. Okay."

"He gave me this."

He reached beyond Scotty to the little Rambler's small glove compartment and retrieved a small black paperback. It had letters on the front cover—obviously Russian letters. Scotty responded as would be expected.

"I can't read Russian."

"Of course. I know. It's Russian for New Testament."

An electrifying jolt went through Scotty's frame. He froze. Did this Russian kitchen worker know about Brandon Marks? Were they friends? Were they at Camp Chalutzim to win converts? No, that couldn't be right. Boris worked there, and Brandon was a camper. They were from two totally different continents, let alone worlds.

"You tell no one."

"Okay, if you say so."

"Okay. But…I believe this book. It is good book. I put it away now."

He returned it to the Nash Rambler's small glove compartment. Scotty thought it best not to mention Brandon Marks, at least not yet.

"We are here now."

He pulled through the gates. And up to Scotty's cabin.

"You tell no one."

As he exited the Rambler, Scotty saw no need to speak further. He simply nodded. And before he could proceed five feet toward the screen door, there was Shlomo waiting for him. His voice had a stressed edge. His eyes expressed something beyond stress—in fact, irritation bordering on outright anger. Like Scotty just minutes before, his arms too were folded.

"It's time to see Rabbi Malmud."

Chapter Thirty-Three

Scotty thought he had used up the one and only strategy—short of secretly calling collect on Malmud's black Bell connection to the civilized world—that would transport him to the single occupancy vacant bedroom he longed for. And even then, he would have to resort to pleading, perhaps even to threatening suicide. Now, he might have the rare opportunity to make his case.

Malmud was on the very instrument of his slim chance when Shlomo and Scotty arrived outside his closed door. Shlomo knocked once, and then knocked two times, as if he was sending a secret signal to the other side. Scotty could hear the muffled elevation of Malmud's excited voice. This continued for another minute or two. Finally, the same voice shouted at the same pitch, but louder.

"Come in."

Shlomo opened the door. Scotty noticed that his face was flushed.

"Rabbi, here he is."

Malmud turned to Scotty, somewhat irritated by the situation. He said the first thing that came to his mind.

"Scotty, I'm responsible for every camper, including you. Do you understand?"

Scotty lowered his head. Shlomo stepped in.

"You see, sir, Scotty here got homesick. He kind of walked off… that is, away from the camp… a little way off."

"I see. Well, Scotty, do you want me to call your parents? I could explain that you were feeling homesick. Maybe you would feel a little less homesick if you talked to them. But I'd like you to stick it out if you could, instead of making them come all the way up here. Tell me, is there anything in particular…any one in particular…that you are having problems with?"

Scotty had no intention of sharing his private secret with this nosy camp director—a secret that the whole cabin was now in on. The "naked" adolescent reality that every pubescent camper of either sex seemed to share, except him, was no business of Malmud's. The rabbi continued.

"There's just two more weeks. Do you want me to call them, so you could just speak to them for a few minutes?"

Rabbi Malmud didn't want to break his record of retaining the campers whose parents had paid significant sums to send them to Camp Chalutzim, particularly those who had more than one child at the camp. The exception, of course, was Billy Bitner. But that was unavoidable and tragic. He left camp on a stretcher, never to return.

"No, thanks. That's okay."

Faced with two weeks remaining in his Chalutzim prison sentence, he left the director's office and headed for the *Fortress of Solitude*, and the imaginary tournament in which he was the hero of the plantain weed championship.

When he arrived at the Fortress, he was pleased that no one was there. After all, solitude was the original reason he chose this very location. This is where he wished he could stay for the remainder of his time away from home, if he had to stay anywhere. In short, The *Fortress of Solitude* was the only bearable spot in this unbearable camp. There, he could feel the sweet summer breeze that fluttered and glided like a dove of peace.

The distant roar of a jet forged a trail thousands of feet above him. That would carry him home faster than any car. But neither jet, nor automobile, nor hitchhiking thumb, were available to him now.

Scotty stood motionless, considering these impossible options. Finally, he decided to face the firing squad. He waited in the Fortress all afternoon shooting plantains until he knew that everyone had left for dinner. He was getting quite good at the *sport*. If only that was an actual activity. He might even win a cheap plastic trophy.

He finally left the Fortress only due to hunger pangs. The prayer before the meal, the motzi, had already been spoken. Everyone was engaged in passing one dish after another around the table. He took his usual place. Malcolm Berman turned to him as his pudgy hands passed the wilted pale broccoli.

"Where have *you* been?"

Scotty sort of lied and sort of told the emotional truth.

"I haven't been feeling too good...but I'm okay now."

"Don't get too close. I don't want to get your cooties."

The word cooties was a "trigger" word for endless teasing. Scotty wanted to squelch that right away before the word itself spread like a contagion.

"No. It's not like that. I'm feeling fine. I'm just a little not myself. I've got a lot on my mind."

"What could you possibly have on your mind? You sound like my mother. She worries and eats—eats and worries."

"Yeah, I guess she *is* a little fat."

Scotty had seen her during the first day of camp. He had thought that but said nothing. Now he was sure he had sparked an argument. But Malcolm just agreed.

"Yeah, like a house."

Suddenly, what was obviously Robert Jonas' rifle went off several times. Startled, Brandon spoke.

"Dinnertime? It's a bit late for target practice."

There was perhaps five seconds of silence, followed by a shriek that brought all passing and even chewing to a frozen pause.

Shlomo spoke an "unacceptable for camp" word.

"What the hell is that?"

Chapter Thirty-Four

For the second time that summer, Scotty heard the increasing volume of sirens, this time accompanied by sporadic honking. One siren joined another, and then another. Scotty dropped his fork and jumped up, pulling his legs out of the bench seat and away from the table. Shlomo called to him.

"Scotty! Where are you going?"

Scotty saw no obligation to respond. He was already halfway home in his mind, and he didn't care what kind of discipline he was in for. What was the worst they could do to him? Send him home? He was more than ready for that. Something was wrong, and he needed to be wherever it was happening. He broke into a run.

By the time he arrived at the Jonas house, the ambulance was parked outside and the emergency team was already inside. He was filled with dread that his worst fears would be confirmed. But would it be Tricia, or Margaret, or...Mack? The door was open, and Scotty marched right in, only to be blocked by a policeman who was standing in the front hallway. He was about as tall as Fred Gwynne of *Car 54, Where Are You?* It had just gone off the air a year earlier.

"Where are you going, son?"

"I have a friend in there."

"You can't come in."

"Is he okay? I mean…"

"I don't know. I wouldn't tell you if I did. Go home, and you'll hear something later."

Another siren slowly increased in volume, and then another. Scotty tried to peer into the house.

"Go home!"

He wanted to shout back: *this isn't home!* But just then, Malmud and two office staff workers pushed past him and entered the house, forcing him away from the entrance and to the edge of the property. Scotty felt helpless. Then, two emergency workers walked out of the house with a stretcher bearing Mack, who seemed to be unconscious. Instinctively, Scotty shouted, "Mack! Mack!" Tricia exited the house. She was white as a Camp Chalutzim Shabbat tablecloth, and obviously in shock. Margaret followed her out, along with one of the office workers.

Mack turned toward Scotty's voice and opened his eyes. He looked right at him. Scotty suddenly began to cry.

"Mack! Mack!"

Within another thirty seconds, the ambulance containing Mack and Tricia, along with two police vehicles, spun their tires and exited the house. Their sirens began to fade, along with Scotty's hope of ever seeing Mack again.

For the first time he noticed Robert, in handcuffs and being escorted by two other officers more the size of Joe E. Ross of the same *Car 54* TV situation comedy. He also looked like he was in shock. But it was a different kind of shock than Tricia's, more like the culpable expression on the face of the infamous Lee Harvey Oswald of the previous November.

Rabbi Malmud exited the house. He also looked shaken. Scotty looked back to see Boris standing a short distance away. Scotty felt unexpectedly drawn to him. He slowly started walking towards him. Scotty had never been overtly affectionate with his own father. And that kind of thing didn't come naturally to him. But in a move surprising even to him, he picked up his pace to a sprint and then ran into Boris's arms, staying there for at least a minute or even two. Tears ran down his face. A fearful thought entered his mind and wouldn't leave. Would Mack go the way of Billy Bitner? Scotty felt the helplessness increase. All the embarrassment that summer over his baby boy body seemed so out of sync with such grown-up emotions. The two experiences seemed incongruous. But then again, so did much of his experience that summer of 1964. It could truly be expressed in three words contained in a top grossing film that had been released on July 11th, in the middle of his enslavement—*A Hard Day's Night*. And it was the darkest night his young life had yet experienced.

Chapter Thirty-Five

Rabbi Malmud had made every effort to assure the Camp Chalutzim children's parents that their offspring were in the best of hands. And the police had supported the camp staff in that regard, even when difficult circumstances arose. Doris and Stan Malnick were thankful to spend a quiet peaceful summer away from Scotty, knowing that he would be home shortly, and about the frantic business of getting ready for another school year. There would be last minute shopping for everything from pens and pencils to shirts and slacks.

It was on such a placid lox, bagel, and cream cheese morning that Stan was imbibing his Maxwell House coffee as he perused the Sunday paper. He generally liked to cover pretty much all of it, from the headlines, through the op ed pages, and finally concluding with Dick Tracy and friends in the comic section. It was somewhere between Ann Landers and the local news that he spotted a tiny article titled, "Trouble at Jewish summer youth camp in the Poconos."

As soon as he saw the words *Chalutzim* and *Malmud*, he shouted several times, increasing the volume with each shout.

"Doris, Doris, **Doris**!"

She was just around the corner in the den. She stood up and bolted into the kitchen.

"What's the matter? Are you okay?"

"Look at this! Just look at this!"

She read a few lines, and then turned pale. When she found her voice, it was shaking.

"That's...there...there...that's...where...Scotty is. It's horrible!"

"You're damn right it is! What are they hiding from us?"

Stan got up and went over to the bulletin board next to the wall phone. There, along with various numbers penciled and penned on various scraps of paper, was Rabbi Malmud's personal office phone number. He grabbed the kitchen phone receiver off the wall and dialed the camp office. The office phone rang. One ring, two rings, three rings, four rings.

"He's refusing to answer, the idiot," Stan fumed.

In addition to her own fear, Doris had to contend with her husband's simmering rage. To do that, she needed to play the executive chef and prevent his anger from boiling over. She despised that job because it came with the risk of getting burned. Nevertheless, she knew she had to say something—anything.

"Stan. When he *does* answer, don't say something you'll regret. We don't know all the details yet."

Stan dropped his spoon into his coffee cup, pushed his chair back, and began pacing back and forth about the length of the cord. Doris went over to the cupboard and grabbed eight Oreos to temporarily allay the stress. If either Doris or Stan had been thinking clearly, they would have realized that Menachem Malmud was likely not contactable because he was at the hospital.

Likewise, anxiously pacing at the *Fortress of Solitude* just before lunch, Scotty figured Mack to be at the same hospital where Billy was taken, and where he died. After all, it was probably the only hospital within several miles. Scotty had to see him. Mack would have done the same for him, if he had been the one who was badly hurt. But he had decided against risking his life hitchhiking again. Once in an enclosed speeding projectile on wheels with a teen maniac was enough. There was only one way to visit his friend. He walked over to the *chadar ha-o-chel*. The main room was empty and quiet. But he could smell lunch's fare—which he guessed was kosher hot dogs—under preparation in the kitchen. He unceremoniously walked in, and there before a huge boiling kettle was Boris.

"Boris, I know I've been a real pain, trying to run away and everything. I feel bad you had to come get me. And I hate to bug you again, but I have a big favor to ask you. Ever since I saw Mack Jonas being taken away in the ambulance the other day, I knew I had to go see him. I should have gone already. But I can't get out of this prison. You're the only one who can help me."

Boris looked him in the eye, and then shook his head back and forth as if he had already decided against it.

"I don't think Rabbi Malmud would want you doing that."

"So why does he need to know?"

"Because I don't want to lose my job, Scotty. That's why."

"Fine. I'll go see him. And he'd *better* let you take me."

"If you talk to him with that attitude, you can forget it."

"I hate him, but I'll play nice."

"Don't hate. Not good for you."

Scotty walked out of the *chadar ha-o-chel* and straight up the path to the office. He opened the yawning screen door and purposely let it slam closed. He remembered the meeting with the director after his fight with Benny. Menachem Malmud didn't impress him then, and he impressed him even less now. The same office worker who embarrassed him the one time he used the bathroom was there. Why wouldn't she be? Startled, she scowled as she stared at him.

"I'm here to see Malmud."

"You mean *Rabbi* Malmud."

"He's not my rabbi. I mean Malmud."

"Young man, you…"

Scotty burst right through the director's door. Just as startled, he began to rise.

"Scotty, can I help you?"

"I understand I need some kind of pass to leave this place and visit my friend Mack in that hospital down the road. And if I don't get it, I'll find a way to visit him anyway."

Without hesitating, the rabbi calmly said, "Why would I deprive you of a mitzvah, Scotty?"

Scotty didn't expect that response. He hesitated, and then said, "Well…good."

"In fact, I'll take you there and I'll visit him with you."

"Well, I don't know if Mr. Jonas would like that."

"What's there not to like?"

"Well, fine then."

Suddenly, another idea crossed Scotty's mind.

"Could we take my close friend with us?"

"And who is that?"

Without hesitating, he responded, "Brandon Marks."

Rabbi Malmud wasn't sure why Scotty wanted Brandon with them. He hoped it didn't have anything to do with the book in Brandon's dresser. Nevertheless, he agreed with a nod.

Chapter Thirty-Six

Scotty was looking very much forward to visiting Mack. He was so relieved that he was apparently improving. But he wasn't at all excited about the entourage that ended up squeezed into Malmud's 1963 compact Dodge Dart. A more disparate crew could not have occupied the seats. It included the director, Brandon, Scotty, Tricia Jonas, and Gus Simmons. The rabbi's prayer book was stowed in his glove compartment for just such occasions. Scotty was sandwiched in the middle of the front bench seat, with his left elbow in the way of the floor shift.

The short trip seemed to pass in slow motion. Scotty could see the hospital in the distance, a medical Oz towering over the Pocono range. As it came closer, Scotty experienced a particularly sharp pang of homesickness, brought on by the highway reaching longingly beyond the farthest hill to the vacant bedroom anxiously waiting for him at home. But at this moment, just beyond the next hill, there was an occupied room to visit, with a metal-framed hospital bed.

The hospital elevator carried not only the five pilgrims, but also two nurses and a doctor. There was continued silence there, as the elevator stopped to let out one nurse, then the other, then the doctor, and finally Rabbi Malmud, Brandon, Tricia, Gus, and Scotty. That was a large group.

Scotty learned later that the rabbi had obtained permission beforehand.

When they finally entered the double occupancy room, Mack was lying on his back, covered with a sheet. He seemed to be awake but at the same time seemed like he wasn't. He opened his eyes partially, then shut them, then opened them partially again. Scotty looked over at the other bed and saw another boy there. He was more alert, and curious about Mack's visitors. Rabbi Malmud broke the silence with small talk.

"How are you boys feeling?"

He was trained to be sensitive to the other patients, particularly children.

Mack breathed a quiet "Okay, sir" to the rabbi. He had seen plenty of yarmulkes at Camp Chalutzim. The other boy in the room knew no Jews, and he had only seen the red caps on Catholic cardinals. However, his mother had taught him to be tolerant of other religions. Still, he felt the awkwardness associated with being the stranger among them. The rabbi sensed that.

"You both look like you're coming along. Well, do you mind if I recite a traditional prayer for healing?"

Scotty felt embarrassed by this display of Jewish tradition in front of the strange boy, and even in front of Mack. It was usually reserved for the privacy of family Chanukah candle lightings and Passover seders. Brandon felt awkward too. He was acutely aware of the clash of religious cultures, and somehow it made him feel put on the spot. Malmud began the traditional Mi Shabeirach prayer.

"Mi Shabeirach Avoteinu, M'Kor Hab'rachah l'moteinu. May the Source of strength who blessed the ones before us, help us find the courage to make our lives a blessing, and let us say, Amen."

Scotty didn't expect to feel any sea-parting power, any energy. Indeed, the prayer didn't seem to be about answers beyond resignation and acceptance of what is or appears to be.

After more friendly small talk, the visit was at an end. But Scotty didn't want to leave. Something stirring deep within him felt an unusual need to do something more. While there was a sliver of time left, Scotty impulsively mouthed unexpected words with enough breath for everyone to just hear them.

"God…Lord…please…heal my friend…please…in Your name.. in…in…"

Then quieter, but still detectable.

"Jesus name…Amen."

The silence became even more silent—if that were possible. Then he turned around 180 degrees and walked past everyone and out of the hospital room.

Chapter Thirty-Seven

The stressful pilgrimage to Mack's hospital bedside drained Scotty. He couldn't wait to exit the oppressive humid air blowing through the cranked-down windows of the cramped Dodge Dart. After Menachem Malmud pulled up beside the office and everyone got out, Scotty knew exactly where to go. He headed toward the one place where he could find silence almost as golden as the bedroom that occupied many of the dreams he had been abruptly awakening from.

Not long after the *Fortress of Solitude* plantain program commenced, it was interrupted by a "special announcement" in the *still* small Voice.

You don't have to feel intimidated before the other boys. Like the plantain, you will bloom physically.

Just when Scotty was about to berate himself for the immature idiocy of his self-talk, the voice added two words that he was sure he wouldn't think up himself.

And spiritually.

Where did *that* come from?

Late that night, during his frankly obsessive privacy-driven bathroom routine, Scotty stared at his weary eyes. From there, he scanned the rest of his tired tanned face. He noticed for the first time, the clear yet shadowy form of a mustache. He gazed back into his own eyes, and then went over to the toilet. He wished he could do more than just pee, but it was too soon after dinner for that. Maybe that would have to wait until everyone else was at breakfast. He was so tired of this routine of constant shame. Then, as he continued to look down, he noticed the beginning of developing pubic hair. He wished it would grow overnight into something matching the other boys. But he was fully cognizant that nature took its time. It was a slowpoke, like him.

Chapter Thirty-Eight

Scotty awakened the next morning expecting the usual predawn dread accompanying the clandestine dressing ritual. And for a few minutes, he experienced it. Then, realizing—or at least trusting—that the scant evidence of pubic hair somehow acted as a shield against naked embarrassment, he shed his pajamas for a brief eternity. He was relieved that no one commented. Simultaneously with that, Malcolm Berman boldly "unsheathed" his wet-tipped towel like a gleaming white sword and began flicking the legs of other similarly unclad campers. Within a millisecond, the cabin was rife with terrycloth swordplay. All the boys, and even Shlomo, partook in the action. That is, all except Scotty, who took the opportunity to don his underwear, pants, and t-shirt. He hoped perhaps now his last several days would be shame free.

The early morning swashbuckling stirred a hunger for breakfast that outpaced the quality of the food. He suddenly realized that it was time to present his new masculine maturity to Sandy Singer. No matter who her latest flame was, Scotty hoped he was man enough to sweep her off her feet. He made sure to race out of the Shacharit service, beating everyone to the *chadar ha-o-chel*. He planned to seat himself right next to her. But when he arrived, a tall boy two years his senior was already dishing out scrambled eggs to the obliging curly-headed Jagger-faced beauty. Scotty summoned his new-found confidence and tapped the boy's shoulder from behind, speaking gently, as befit the occasion.

"I know it's an imposition, but do you mind moving over a bit so I can kind of squeeze myself in there?"

The boy spoke while turning around.

"Buzz off, squirt."

The whole table looked toward him in silence that contrasted with the crosstalk throughout the hall. Scotty knew he had to either hold his ground or lose his chance to win Sandy. His competition was losing patience.

"Don't you belong at another table, squirt?"

Suddenly, the boy swung fully around and grabbed Scotty, throwing him onto the concrete floor like a ventriloquist's dummy. Red, furious, and tossing all caution overboard, Scotty grabbed the boy's white sock-clad leg and pulled him off-balance so swiftly that he fell to the floor, cracking his head so hard that everyone within twenty feet could hear it. Not content with that, Scotty leaned down and punched him squarely on the nose like Ralphie punched Scott Farkus in the film *A Christmas Story*. And just like in that adaptation of Jean Shepherd's short story, the boy's nose bled. But in this case, it didn't break. That is not to say that it wouldn't be black and blue for at least a few days.

Not quite in time, Rabbi Malmud ran over from the counselors' table and grabbed Scotty's arm before he inflicted more serious damage. He had to exert serious muscle power to restrain the rage-fueled appendage. The "victim" howled like a wounded hound, and then cupped his nose as he began screaming uncontrollably. The rabbi turned to Scotty, gritted his teeth, and spoke through them.

"When I'm through here, meet me in my office."

Scotty wanted to curse Malmud out using the foulest language he knew. But instead, he sucked in air and then angrily exhaled. Then he stomped out, purposely slamming the screen door violently. The rabbi looked around at the stunned assemblage, realizing he had to say something to try to address the situation.

"All right everyone. It's over. Go back to your breakfast before it gets cold. Boris, please take Jacob to the infirmary. I'll be there shortly."

Then he left the building through the same screen door. Scotty wanted to seek refuge in the *Fortress of Solitude*, but he realized that some hired grunt or other would go after him. He just stood outside the office and breathed fire with silent moving lips.

"If I could just leave this unkosher...disgusting, claptrap... hypocritical...totally rotten place right now. But I tried that already. When I get out of this jail, I never want to see it or that worthless Malmud again." His straw-dogging was a convenient rehearsal for the real thing. He was interrupted by Malmud, who came to the screen door, accompanied by his secretarial assistant.

"Mr. Malnick, could you please step into my office?"

Scotty marched in like a rebellious prisoner in a German Stalag.

Rabbi Malmud walked in and proceeded to recline in his office chair with his legs stretched out and his clad feet propped up on the desk. He turned to one of the secretaries.

"Please go get Lilly from the *chadar ha-o-chel* and ask her to head for the infirmary to assist with the situation there." Then he turned back to Scotty.

"Mr. Malnick, your parents will be charged the full amount of any damages associated with Jacob's injury. And my staff will discuss further charges and your camp status."

Scotty wasn't familiar with legal language, but he knew that the director was using jargon he'd heard Raymond Burr use on TV's Perry Mason. He might as well have been watching a TV show back home in the den of his familiar house, complete with a bowl of popcorn. He couldn't care less what his parents would be charged or what his status was—unless it was ejection from the camp. He was all for that.

"You may go back and finish your breakfast. That's all."

Just then, an office staff worker rushed in, out of breath and obviously upset.

"There's an episode of some sort happening near the front gate."

The rabbi stood up.

"I'm on my way."

Chapter Thirty-Nine

When Rabbi Malmud reached the gate, there was anything but solitude happening just feet from Scotty's beloved Fortress. Ralph Messer, Richard Starks, and other charter members of the Purple Patriots were standing nose to nose with Robert Jonas, who had just been released from custody on probation. Normally, Robert would be standing *with* them, but he had decided that it was wiser to stand with Mack's friends at Camp Chalutzim instead, and to distance himself from the Purple Patriots. Rabbi Malmud was acting in his role as a clerical peacemaker, although his kippah might just as well have represented an Israeli Defense Forces beret, or a red flag before a raging bull. The tension increased every second, like brittle tinder on an arid day. The static spark occurred when Messer's nose just brushed against Robert's.

Messer struck first, with a jab to the gut and a sneering "You Jew-loving hypocrite!" Robert struck back by regaining his balance and slapping Messer hard across his face. Richard Starks then yanked the rabbi's kippah off his head, simultaneously spitting on and stomping on it.

Once again, sirens in the distance grew increasingly louder. Boris, having received word from the camp gate while cooking dinner in his kitchen, had called for help. When the police cruiser arrived, screeching to a halt, the doors flew open, and the two familiar officers emerged.

"All right, everyone! Cease and desist right now! Break it up! And if you come back to this camp for any reason whatsoever, we'll take you all in and book you. I don't care *who* you are, and *what* your beef is."

Messer, Starks, and the other Purple Patriots backed away, with daggers in their eyes and gritted teeth. Robert turned to Rabbi Malmud with a newfound softness even he didn't expect.

"Thank you, Rabbi...for trying to help."

Menachem Malmud extended his hand to him as the Purple Patriot members backed up one by one, like the adulteress's accusers in John 8. As they left, waving their hands in disgust, Robert Jonas firmly grasped the rabbi's hand.

"Thank *you*, Robert."

Scotty was just arriving at the Fortress ready to witness fireworks, only to find it occupied by the director and Mack's father. He missed the opportunity to display his newly budding masculine strength. Brandon Marks followed close behind. They both left the Fortress and walked the path back to their cabin.

Shlomo and Lilly were missing in action during the entire skirmish between Robert Jonas and the Purple Patriots. They were outside the gate and just far enough down the road to hold hands firmly and unselfconsciously.

As they slowly strolled, Shlomo felt free to share his thoughts openly.

"Lilly, I could use some sage advice."

"What about?"

"Well...it's about this boy in my cabin. You know him. After all, everybody knows everybody."

Lilly stopped and turned to Shlomo.

"Let me guess. It's Brandon Marks."

"How'd you guess?"

"Like you said, everybody knows everybody."

"So, what do I do about his Bible with the New Testament, and his...well, his faith."

"So how open is he about it?"

"I don't know. Everyone in the cabin knows."

"So does he...proselytize?"

"*That's* a big theological word."

"You don't know what it means?"

"Of *course*, I know."

"So *does* he?"

"Well, not exactly."

"Then what's the problem?"

"For one thing, it's a Jewish camp. What would my grandparents think?"

"Who cares what they think?"

"You mean would think...if they were alive. You see, they died at the hands of Nazis, in a *Christian* country."

"Well, it seems to me that Brandon Marks is not only harmless; he's the farthest thing from a Nazi."

Shlomo stopped and turned to Lilly.

"Well, it's getting late. And everyone will be wondering where we are."

Lilly nodded in agreement. Then they turned and headed back to Camp Chalutzim.

Chapter Forty

Scotty lay exhausted on his paper-thin mattress, on his bony wire frame bed, in the cold-steam-breath grey chill of the final week at Camp Chalutzim. The word *finally* fit better than merely *final*. He could scarcely believe the two-month-or-so incarceration was almost at its end. Soon the buses would be lined up outside the cabins, with their undercarriage doors lifted high like gull wings ready to whisk their precious adolescent cargo back to civilization.

Scotty could now just make out something he couldn't quite discern in the crack of a final dawn. It must have been there when he went to sleep. Or was it? An old newspaper clip picture of the four girls murdered at a Birmingham, Alabama church the prior September was taped to his bureau. And written in bright red ink across the bottom of the photo were the words "YOU'RE NEXT!"

Scotty rubbed his eyes. Was he seeing right or was the message just a blurry apparition? He had never been threatened like this before. True, he had been needled by a boy in his class who was so short that it was obvious even to Scotty that there was no threat. He realized that the boy was trying to gain stature he didn't literally possess. But this was something different—something more threatening.

The morning was taken up with more camp drama, complete with one officer (that would suffice this time), Rabbi Malmud, and Scotty. The officer tried to calm everyone.

"When we see threats like this, we take them seriously. However, it's very rare when they are acted upon. Nevertheless, we err on the side of caution. Of course, we've contacted your parents, Scotty, and they're on their way up here."

Scotty immediately felt a sudden rumbling tension begin from the esophageal side of his stomach all the way to the intestinal side. He dreaded the expected flash of his father's anger. He was sure it was intensifying mile by mile as he and Doris approached the camp.

When they finally arrived and got out of the familiar family car, his father stepped in front of his mother and took an unexpected lead as he approached director Malmud.

"Rabbi, if you can't keep those back-hills rednecks away from my son, you'll be hearing from my lawyer!"

Malmud tried speaking in his rabbinic "steadying" tone.

"I'm sure if we put our heads together…"

"You keep my head out of it!"

"I'm trying…"

A growing crowd of campers began to form around Stan Malnick and Menachem Malmud. The rabbi realized that defusing in this case was useless. Lilly went over and grabbed Shlomo's hand. Then she whispered in his ear.

"*Do* something, Shlomo. Counselors are supposed to counsel. Well…do some counseling. This is terrible for Scotty…and everyone."

Shlomo knew Lilly expected more of him, and he knew he should be the man and play the mediator. But he hadn't yet figured out how.

Scotty was too embarrassed about his father's behavior to step in. He was experiencing a paralysis that disenabled the budding man with the subtle stubble. And all his mother could do was quietly repeat, "Stan, don't. Don't."

It was up to Brandon Marks to play the peacemaker of Sermon on the Mount note.

"If I may interject, Mr. Malnick...Rabbi Malmud...don't you think we should focus our energy on finding the sick person who wrote this? After all, he threatened one of our campers."

Aware of Brandon's barely tolerable religious views, Scotty's father interjected.

"You're the *last* one to talk! You shouldn't even *be* at this camp!"

Lilly felt a pressing need to jump in and support Brandon. Her habit of defending the oppressed assumed an atypical form usually more reminiscent of a Jewish response to church anti-Semitism.

"I think I can speak for the whole Camp Chalutzim staff when I say that everyone is welcome here—Reform, Conservative, Orthodox, Reconstructionist, and even those outside of those expressions."

Stan Malnick shot back, "But not so-called Jewish-Christians!"

That remark left everyone momentarily speechless. Scotty could feel his racing heartbeat in his neck and chest at the same time. He knew he had to respond. Finally, he haltingly responded.

"Dad...um...Brandon...um...he's my friend...my good friend. You shouldn't be talking to my friend that way."

Doris took a deep breath and spoke softly but with a clipped edge.

"I agree with Scotty, Stan. We didn't raise our children to talk that way. And Scotty knows that."

"So now you're siding with these lunatics. I didn't pay good money to expose my son to crazy missionaries. Let's go right now!"

He turned to Menachem.

"I want a full refund, plus expenses for damages to my family's reputation and well-being."

Doris put her hands on her hips and stomped her right foot once.

"I'm not going *anywhere*, and neither is Scotty. I apologize for my husband's outburst and the embarrassment he's causing. We need to find out who's harassing my son, and frankly, threatening him. And we're not leaving anywhere until we do. Lilly, Shlomo, don't you agree that this is a civil rights issue? You didn't risk your lives in Mississippi only for us to ignore this threat."

They both nodded in assent. The rabbi spoke as emphatically as possible.

"I couldn't agree more. We will get the authorities right on it and keep you posted."

Even as Rabbi Malmud sought to address the danger posed by anti-Semites in the area, he knew there was another danger that was equally dangerous. He never expected "missionary" activity to be discussed in any other forum besides the *anti-missionary* training provided by a certain segment of the Jewish community. He was unprepared for even a subtle form of legitimacy, which he feared was occurring before his eyes. He further realized that all future missionary activity must be shut down immediately, and forbidden for the remainder of the camp year, short as it was. But as long as guitar-toting, protest-loving "Joan Baez" was around, it seemed an impossibility. So, he brainstormed for an instant, and then appealed to Stan.

"Next year, we'll add a question to the application that will resolve this whole matter for good."

He turned to Lilly and read her face with probing eyes. If she agreed even tacitly, the conversation was over. She hesitated for only two to three seconds, which provided the perfect opportunity for him to go in for the kill.

"My secretary will type up what I dictate to her. I have another appointment."

He walked away, quickening his pace as he went. Everyone began to leave. Stan was satisfied with the results of his inconvenient excursion to Camp Chalutzim. He decided he would get his money's worth and leave his son there for the short several days left.

"I think we're finished here. Thank you for your help, Rabbi. I'm satisfied with the results. Behave yourself like a good Jew, Scotty, and we'll see you back home soon. Come on, Doris."

With that, he opened the car door for Doris, and then got in the driver's side. Gravel flew out from under the tires as the car headed for the gate, and the road back to civilization.

Chapter Forty-One

After an early afternoon that left Scotty feeling like a kryptonite-overdosed Superman, he retreated to the one location within the confines of Camp Chalutzim where he could experience some solace—his beloved Fortress. When he arrived, he was pleased that it was unoccupied—just as he hoped. He was in no mood for a game of plantains. His interest in pretending to be a world-famous sportsman had at least temporarily waned.

Instead, Scotty's active imagination could just make out the faint outlines of recording studio walls. He saw in his mind's eye a group of gifted musicians encircling him. He picked up a branch roughly in the shape of a Fender electric guitar—very roughly. He stepped up to an imaginary mic perched on an equally imaginary mic stand. He counted to four and began singing in a Frankie Valli falsetto to the birds and the trees.

"Sa-andy, Sandy Baby, Sa-andy, Sandy Baby, Sa-a-a-a-andy Baby, Sandy Baby."

He continued to strum away on his "six string" branch, while picking out a mean lead every few measures. He kept singing "Sa-andy, Sandy Baby" louder and louder, with an abandon that ended up reaching Ralph Messer's unseen ears. They perked up as he was standing in his small backyard. Not that he needed much of an excuse to attack a teen camper hailing from far off Jewish suburbia. But this one was as good as any. He charged over the camp fence and ran like a bull into an unprepared Scotty, knocking him down. Scotty quickly got up and began running toward the camp offices and *chadar ha-o-chel*. Ralph caught up to him and grabbed him by his sneakers. He pulled him down and proceeded to sit on him while beating on his head, which Scotty shielded with both of his hands.

That caught the attention of Boris who, as always, was busy cooking that night's dinner. He quickly entered the fray. By that time, any camper within a few hundred feet stopped what he or she was doing, with permission or without, and ran in the direction of the melee. They formed another one of those cheering circles, obviously on the side of Boris and Scotty. When Shlomo, Lilly, and even Menachem arrived on the scene, the cheering section was so strong that at least one or two of them were strongly tempted to join in. After all, didn't Ralph Messer and his clearly anti-Semitic friends have this coming? However, Malmud knew what he had to do. He blew the whistle conveniently hanging from his neck so loud that every human and dog within a mile must have heard it. That had the intended effect of causing everyone to freeze in place. During the short pause in hostilities, Boris took the opportunity to walk over to Ralph Messer and give his face an explosive wallop, sending him crashing to the ground and knocking him out cold. The camp director clapped his hands three times.

"That's enough! Boris! What are you doing?"

Boris stood over Messer with his feet parted like the Colossus of Rhodes.

"I learn different in my country. No nice guy to not nice person. Scotty is my friend. If you touch him, I touch you!"

If Scotty was the "Superman" whose *Fortress of Solitude* had been invaded by the diabolical "Lex" Messer, he failed in his mission to repel the supervillain, protect the Fortress, save Camp Chalutzim, and by extension the vulnerable Sandy "Lane"- who at any rate was missing in action on this day. And he was glad she was. He hadn't saved the day, or even a minute of it. That was a job for Boris—a job Scotty had no interest in.

As Menachem Malmud stepped up to Boris to shake his hand, Boris withdrew his.

"I'm sorry, Rabbi. This is not what this Russian dissident is good for. Bad example for children."

"Please. It didn't call for a pacifist."

Ralph Messer struggled into a sitting position and looked up at the assembled group. He struggled for words for several seconds, but they finally came to him.

"You will hear from my lawyer. You will *all* be hearing from my lawyer. *All* of you. Jews and Jew lovers. And the Purple Patriots. You'll hear from them. You'll *more* than hear from them."

A voice from the other side of the fence spoke up.

"What are you doing, threatening these people, Messer?"

It was Robert Jonas, and his son Mack was with him. They breached the fence and drew near.

"The Purple Patriots aren't opposed to a good fist fight. And from where I stood, that's what it looked like, Messer."

Messer snapped back.

"Well…all of you…*all* of you are trespassing on this land. Since this camp was created, it's been trespassing on Christian land as far as I'm concerned…land that my family has lived in for three generations. That's why we need the Purple Patriots. Isn't that right, Jonas? This whole camp has grabbed this land and made a…a little Jew ghetto here. It's an invasion is what it is. And someday we'll get this land back. Anyway, you won't hear the last of me…or *us*."

All of this was very upsetting to Mack, whose face was red with rage.

"My dad and me, we don't see it that way. And my friend Scotty doesn't see it that way. Maybe we can all have it out right here and now. Maybe we don't need the cops. Maybe we just need a good old-fashioned brawl. That's all you jerks understand anyway."

Scotty hesitated, and then muttered a few words to Mack.

"I...I'm not sure, Mack. I've never done that kind of thing."

Malmud interjected.

"Not here and not now! Not on my watch! I'll call in the authorities again and we'll finish this ridiculous, inappropriate episode. Or maybe the state highway patrol."

Shlomo knew the Freedom Rider in him had to speak up, especially with Lilly there.

"If we learned anything in the civil rights movement..."

Now Ralph Messer interjected.

"All Commies! That's all you are!"

Shlomo shot back.

"Shut up, Messer. Now, as I was saying, in the civil rights movement we learned that violence serves nothing. Now I'm going to ask you to go home and cool off. *All* of you. That's enough for today. Perhaps we can discuss your grievances at some point. But of course, we only have a week or less left. This discussion is over now. Please disband. Now."

Ralph Messer cursed under his breath as he walked away. Scotty was glad to have his beloved Fortress back and was also anxious to hear the blessing before the evening meal. He was ready even for bug juice and skinny burgers.

Chapter Forty-Two

Scotty lay in bed after the last Shabbat of the camp summer, considering his infantile frame. Despite his faint mustache and subtle hint of pubic hair, he still lagged far behind every other boy in the cabin. In fact, he lagged far behind either sex, except perhaps Fern. Her body seemed as mousy as her stringy red hair. It hadn't occurred to him that her lack of physical maturity was in any way connected to her insecurity, and her eagerness to proclaim her supposed relationship conquests. Now at the end of his imprisonment, that began to make sense to him. She was his female counterpart. Only it was probably harder on her. He only hoped that the boys' banter had never escaped the thin walls of the boys' wooden cabin.

Sandy is stacked, but Fern is as flat as an ironing board. She doesn't even need a training bra.

When Scotty first overheard such talk from Gus Simmons and Malcolm Berman, he paid scant attention to it. Now he realized the pain that such comments would cause Fern. Of course, the time would come when she would "fill out," even if she'd never be a Jayne Mansfield. But to her, that time was a forever away.

All of this triggered a question that had never occurred to him.

Why would God allow some children to lag behind and stay immature longer than others? In particular, why are some bar mitzvah boys called young men when some are obviously not men at all? The rabbis who officiate their ceremonies don't ever mention that. They just perform that rite as if it's *one size fits all.* Some are little children physically. Some are young adults. But everyone chants the blessings as if being thirteen itself is a joyous rite of passage and not a confusing mess. And here he was away from home, in the middle of it all, trapped between a caterpillar and a butterfly—stuck actually—at Camp Chalutzim, of all places. Well, at least it would all end very soon.

These thoughts acted as an unsettling drone leading to a fitful night's sleep. When the dawn's early light hit the window and reveille hit his ears, Shlomo was standing fully dressed at the front of the cabin.

"Boker Tov, campers! Today Lilly and I will take you on an excursion to meet a very special person who will share her own experiences with us. We've told you about hidden poverty in this region. And you helped those experiencing it. Now she will tell us about hidden prejudice occurring not in the south, but right here near Camp Chalutzim. The bus will be here right after breakfast to take us to our destination."

Everyone in both cabins was curious about a morning excursion so close to the end of the camp year. This was more irritating to Scotty than exciting. He was expecting a short straight line to his home and his bed. This momentary interruption held no fascination for him. He would rather spend the day making clay out of talcum powder and baby shampoo with Brandon Marks or shooting plantains with Mack Jonas.

After an awful breakfast of lumpy oatmeal and powdered eggs, followed by an embarrassing cabin visit to the bathroom with impatient campers waiting outside, Scotty boarded the old loud yellow school bus with girls and boys his age. As usual, boys sat with boys and girls sat with girls. Sandy was across the aisle and two rows behind him. Fern was on his side and two rows in front of him. Brandon was next to him, and Gus was just behind him. It was a short trip to the destination, which appeared to be an old brick church. Everyone piled out and waited outside. Scotty had never been in a church. He looked up at its white spire with a small plain cross on top, then down to the cracked slat building coated with white paint. After a few minutes, everyone piled in.

As soon as he entered the church, he felt a sudden electric chill, and an odd presence that reminded him of the *Fortress of Solitude*. Then he looked past the blonde wooden pews, and up at raised lettering above the dark mahogany pulpit. They spelled out familiar words.

Let your light so shine among men, that they may see your good works, and glorify your Father which is in heaven.

He brought his gaze down again. There, seated in the front row, was a large African American woman in a plain green dress, surrounded by several middle-aged women, some white and some black. Out of an apparent show of respect, Lilly took a seat, followed by Shlomo and Brandon Marks. Scotty wondered what Lilly thought about the words on the wall. They did seem like a coincidence. Was Scotty the only camper who knew where they came from, that they were attributed to none other than the Jesus of Brandon's book?

The woman stood up and walked over to the pulpit, which was off to the side and directly in front of Scotty. She raised her head, which was adorned with a broad silk flowered hat.

"Hello. My name is Mamie. I am the Church Mother of Redemption African Methodist Episcopal Church. Welcome, young Jewish visitors. We are honored to have you with us. You are seated in a church that is playing an important role in the present struggle for our Negro rights. Look around you. These walls reflect the sacrifice that marchers and freedom riders, students and teachers, black and white, Jews and Gentiles, are making today. You are the future of this great nation. Shlomo and Lilly, who have brought you here today, are soldiers in this great battle. The words on the front wall are from the New Testament. You may or may not be familiar with them. There are others in the prophets of Israel that say similar things. Amos tells us to "let justice roll like a river."

As Mamie continued, artificial silk flowers accentuating her hat, Scotty pondered the pervasive presence. It was the same presence that he sensed at the *Fortress of Solitude*. Then that same voice spoke.

Tell Brandon Marks what—or who—you sense.

Scotty responded to his own thoughts.

Why would I do that?

Then another thought came to him, or as crazy as it seemed, through him.

Trust me.

He asked to no one, "Trust who?"

This was certainly nothing but a mental game of conversational imagination. He'd done a lot of that ever since he was perhaps five years old. He tried to ignore the words and listen to the speaker, who had become increasingly boring. But even as her words bled into each other the thought repeated.

Trust me. Tell him.

He tried to throw the question into his cerebral trash can, like a ridiculous idea intentionally forgotten. And for the time being, it seemed to work. By the time Mamie finished admonishing the young troops about their call to action, thoughts about anything he sensed had almost disappeared. Almost.

Chapter Forty-Three

Scotty could hardly believe that there were just three days left until liberation. There would be just two weeks after that before school. But it promised to be an island of complete abandon. He finally resolved that he would never again allow his parents to talk him into any kind of summer camp, no matter what their reasons for doing so. But that was for later. This was now. And he purposed to live joyfully in the now. He even offered thanks through the well-known prayer thanking God for allowing him to reach this season of young adulthood. *Baruch atah Adonai Eloheynu Melech Ha-olam shehechiyanu v'kee-imanu v'higiyanu, lazman hazeh. Blessed are you Lord our God, King of the universe, who has kept us, and preserved us in life, and has allowed us to reach this season.* He was glad he had no immediate responsibilities, other than packing in advance of unpacking—and asking Brandon Marks about what or who he sensed at the *Fortress of Solitude*, and again at the old brick church where Mamie shared.

After a mediocre, overly fishy tuna lunch, Scotty approached Brandon during the free time. Benny was a seriously religious Jew. But Scotty had a question he knew he couldn't answer. Only Brandon could answer the question.

"Brandon, how would you like to take a short walk?"

"What for?"

"Just because."

"Because what?"

"I'll tell you what when we talk."

"OK. OK. I hope I didn't do anything…"

"No, it's nothing like that."

Scotty intentionally walked slowly so he could get all his thoughts out.

"Brandon."

Brandon shared a few of his thoughts first.

"I can't believe that I'll be back home with my mom, and dad, and little brother, and big sister in just a few days. And then back to school."

"You never mentioned them. Weren't they away at camp?"

"They could only afford to send me. My dad says it's been a bad year this year."

"Oh. Well…Brandon?"

"What is it?"

"I think I'm supposed to ask you something."

"About what?"

"Well, about something a little…different. Something hard to explain."

"Okay. But I don't understand. Why doesn't whoever it is that asked you to ask me something just ask me, instead of asking you to ask me?"

"It's not like that. Anyway, did you sort of sense something—or someone—at that church, someone I sensed at the *Fortress of Solitude*? I know it sounds spooky. But then again, not really. I wouldn't ask someone like Rabbi Malmud or anything, or even Shlomo. But maybe it was someone like…like…Jesus or someone?"

Brandon stopped short and turned to Scotty.

"That's the Ruach HaKodesh."

"They may speak Hebrew at Camp Chalutzim, but could you please speak English?"

"If I do, you'll probably think I'm Catholic. But it's in the Tanach."

"Well? Try me."

"The Holy Spirit."

"You're right. You're Catholic."

"Try Psalm 51."

"I'm not trying anything."

"Whatever. You're the one who asked me."

Brandon could sense uneasiness on Scotty's part. He apparently didn't feel comfortable wanting to know what he didn't know, even though down deep he wanted to know what he had sensed. Brandon had had conversations like this before. They were the times when a change in subject was about to occur, as was the case now. Scotty walked ahead. Brandon kept the same slow pace. Loneliness enveloped Scotty like a silent shroud.

Chapter Forty-Four

Ralph Messer was sure of one thing. Whatever Jews like Shlomo or Lilly were, he was the opposite. They were from the filthy ghettos of Communist Russia. His veins ran free with bright red Anglo-Saxon American blood. They represented a Jewish assault on America. He represented the purity of the white race. Even if no one living in this rural community dotted with camps full of invaders perceived the danger, he knew of many true citizens who did. They were the Purple Patriots from chapters near and far.

He had lain awake the last few nights considering a plan. If these left-wing liberal agitators could protest, so could the Patriots. He realized that it would cost the price of several long-distance phone calls, but that would be well worth the price. Secrecy was essential. No one in his family must know what he was planning. There was only one way to assure total privacy. He grabbed his car keys, a small black frayed notebook, and several dimes off the kitchen table, and headed out the back door, quietly shutting it behind him. Then he turned the key in the ignition and backed out of the driveway.

About a quarter mile down the two-lane highway leading to and from Camp Chalutzim was a lone enclosed phone booth. He growled when he saw another parked car near the booth, and an old man in a black fedora hat inside. His plan was momentarily stalled due to "some hick idiot." He was tempted to honk his horn and blast the man out of the booth, but he stopped himself. He used the time by opening the book and studying the names, considering which he'd call first. Finally, the booth squeaked as it opened, and the man headed for his car. Ralph Messer quickly entered the booth and began feeding the phone with dimes, dialing the numbers of various Purple Patriots. He cursed under his breath as the unusually slow dial turned, representing each digit. He knew he had to keep the calls short. He only had so many dimes, and he wanted to inform as many of the members as possible.

Within a half hour, he had tried every number. Some answered and some either didn't, or their phones were busy. But he had reached enough of them to ensure that a sizable group would at least be open to his plan and spread the word to others. He decided to call it a *March on Camp Chalutzim,* named after the *March on Washington* the year before. The march itself would be used primarily to recruit apathetic neighbors, who would then be instrumental in shutting camps like this down. Signs would be used instead of shouting. He believed that would be more effective. It would be a fitting conclusion to Camp Chalutzim summer 1964, which was just a little over a day away.

Chapter Forty-Five

Scotty sat next to Gus at the last lunch of the summer. Just like Scotty, Gus too had changed over the last few months. He seemed a bit thinner, some of the baby fat having been relocated into maybe an inch or so of height. It seemed that everyone had changed somewhat, but it was more obvious with Gus. Benny had changed too. He was not only slightly taller, but he seemed to look more like a young yeshiva student than a little smooth-faced Chassidic school boy.

Scotty knew he had to visit the *Fortress of Solitude* one last time, more to spend some quiet time alone saying goodbye than to shoot plantains. Perhaps he would never do that again now that he was growing up. As he entered the only true oasis in the lonely desert that was Camp Chalutzim, he was unexpectedly greeted by that gentle voice and quiet presence whose identity he had to admit he knew.

Now you will be going home. There will be one more challenge. Meet it as the man you professed to be months ago.

Scotty knew that meant his bar mitzvah. He never believed that made him a man. In fact, getting all those presents made him feel more like a birthday boy. But he sensed this was different, and something about it frightened him. If what he was hearing was coming from something outside his own imagination, then what did it mean?

When Scotty returned from lunch, he discovered the meaning. Standing inches from the camp gate was a large crowd of what looked like local people. He recognized one man. He forgot his name. But others who were whispering among themselves reminded him. Ralph Messer. Mack was nowhere in sight. Brandon had caught up with Scotty. And Boris was already there.

"I don't like looks of this. Where is Malmud?"

The protesters, if that's what they were, were eerily silent. Signs on thin wooden slats they were holding high spoke for them.

Intruders

Jews go home

Christians only here

Scotty knew immediately what he had to do. He turned to Brandon.

"Get your New Testament. Hurry!"

"Are you crazy?"

"Just get it. Please. Now!"

Brandon left. Scotty turned to Boris.

"I've seen you with a bullhorn for getting campers' attention. I need it right now."

Boris hesitated.

"Please, Boris."

"I hope you know what you're doing because I'm sure Rabbi Malmud won't like it. And he won't be happy with me either."

Scotty looked him in the eye. An unexplainable boldness overwhelmed him.

"I know what I'm doing, Boris."

Boris immediately left for the *chadar ha-o-chel* and came back with the horn. Scotty knew that the verse he had heard in the folk song was in the first part of the book, in the fifth chapter. It was one of the few

New Testament verses he knew. As soon as Brandon returned, he thumbed through the pages. Then he lifted the horn and squeezed the trigger.

"This is for you, Ralph Messer. 'Let your light so shine before men, that they may see your good works, and glorify your Father which is in heaven.'"

Messer turned toward him and forced a mocking laugh.

"Don't quote to *me* from your Jewish book. And gimme that horn!"

At least that got his attention. Scotty tossed the horn to Boris and shouted as loudly as he knew how.

"That's in the New Testament. Jesus was Jewish! I guess you hate Him too!"

Ralph walked up to Scotty, drew back his fist, and hit him squarely on the nose. Scotty fell to the ground and covered his nose with his hand. Fresh red blood oozed between his fingers. Humiliation and rage combined in Scotty like the combustible elements of rocket fuel. He tried to get up but faltered. Boris grabbed his shoulders from behind and held him in his muscular Russian arms.

"You go now, Mr. Messer. I deal with you later."

As the sound of sirens once again increased in the thick August air, Ralph Messer suddenly realized he had crossed a boundary by striking a minor. He turned to the restless mob behind him.

"We've…we've made our point. Let's go."

Boris had other plans for them.

"You go nowhere. The cops almost here. Chickens run. You stay, or I make sure they visit all your houses. My cooks give them pictures they have been taking from new Kodak Instamatics."

Sure enough, two cooks stood at the *chadar ha-o-chel* steps snapping pictures. The infirmary doors slammed as the nurse ran toward the scene. To Scotty, it all seemed slow motion and out of body, as if he was watching it unfold from high on some motion picture crane. But the *Voice* wasn't remote. It was just a slim sixteenth of an inch from each ear, as if in the latest stereophonic sound.

I love your enemy. You love him, too.

There was no need to question the Voice. Instantly and unexpectedly, tangible love like warm honey poured all over Scotty. The nurse quickly checked his nose. She sighed a sigh of relief and placed an ice-filled napkin in Scotty's hand. He put the napkin on his nose as he lifted his eyes to behold Ralph Messer. All he could see was a sick body riddled with a spiritual kind of cancer. It took the wind out of his lungs and left him breathless. Warm tears trickled down his cheeks. Of course, he knew that not one person understood why—no one but the One who suffered the rage of enemies and uttered the words his inner ears heard.

His inner voice responded, *Okay, I will.* Like one thought following on the close heels of another, the *Voice* responded.

Then today you are truly a man.

The police pulled up, with sirens turned off. They exited the car, as Rabbi Malmud arrived, along with Shlomo and Lilly. One of the policemen approached Scotty.

"You okay, son? What happened here?"

"I just hurt my nose. I'm fine. Not very convenient on the last day of camp. But thankfully it's not broken."

"We heard it may be something more."

"No. I'm fine."

Scotty glanced over at Ralph Messer and then at Boris again, who glanced back knowingly. The policeman who had been dealing with disruptions since the defacing problem earlier in the summer pulled out his handcuffs. They gleamed in the sunlight. He turned to Ralph Messer.

"Give me your wrists. I'm taking you in."

"For what, officer? It's a free country, and our signs are off the camp property."

"For disrupting the peace around here, and whatever else the judge determines. I've had enough of you and your stupid Purple Patriots. This won't happen again next year."

Messer stiffened.

"We have a constitutional right to protest. We haven't trespassed or broken any other law. We know our rights."

"As they say, tell it to the judge. Okay, folks. This show is over. Break it up. And get rid of those signs."

Chapter Forty-Six

The final morning dawned promising a cloudless, sunny, late summer day. There was dew on the wooden railings of the cabins. But that would evaporate shortly. Everyone was standing outside next to the buses with their camp trunks. The usual business of saying goodbye was in process. Most of the girls were crying and hugging each other, as if they were grieving a death. But, of course, it would be short-lived. By that evening, they would be telling stories over a home-cooked meal with their respective families.

The boys were more stoic. Scotty, his black and blue nose covered with a small band-aid, moved quickly from Gus, to Benny, to Brandon, to Fern, to Sandy, and even to counselors Shlomo and Lilly. He specifically took Brandon aside.

"Um…do you think you'll be back next year?"

That wasn't what he had in mind to say, but it was a quick door opener.

"I think so. How about you?"

"I don't know. Um…I just wanted to say…"

He stalled, what with so many campers and counselors around.

"Yes?"

"Well…I just wanted to say that…I learned a lot…or anyway, some things…about, you know…"

He lowered his voice and came close.

"About…the J person. You know."

"I'm glad you read some of my…my book."

Scotty blushed.

"I learned things I never knew before."

Brandon betrayed a thin smile. When all the goodbyes were exhausted, everyone boarded their buses. As Scotty's bus gently descended the spiraling Pocono Mountains, he looked out at the bushes in the foreground, the trees in the midground, and the sprawling farmland in the background, like the various planes on the Multiplane camera in a Disney cartoon classic. But this wasn't a child's view. This was a young man's journey from near to far, and back to near again—but a different near, a different perspective. He sat next to Gus, wondering what he was thinking. Was he looking forward to being back home with his family?

There was one thing for sure that Scotty was looking forward to. He had missed the privacy of his bedroom. But the Scotty that would occupy that familiar space was an older Scotty, a taller Scotty, a more physically mature Scotty, a whole different Scotty. Would the room feel the same?

When the bus finally reached its destination, and he disembarked, there were his mother and father, and the familiar Pontiac station wagon. Most everyone had already said their goodbyes. They were busy hugging family members and transferring luggage to cars. After helping put his camp trunk into the rear of the wagon, Scotty simply said he was tired. Then he slipped into the clear plastic seat-covered back seat, and promptly fell into a deep sleep. Two months of the social stress of shame and strangers began to fall away.

But what had he learned? How had he changed? Perhaps his first dinner at home would give some indication. Doris broke the ice that evening.

"My, you've grown even in the last month, Scotty. You're really growing up."

He wasn't sure how to respond to that.

"Really?"

She had cooked his favorite dish, breaded veal cutlet with spaghetti and tomato sauce. Stan was more inquisitive.

"So, what did they teach you?"

"I don't know."

"I hope it strengthened your ties with the Jewish community."

"I guess so."

Stan was losing patience, as he often did.

"So, what about the hick Jew haters near the camp, and the Jewish Christian they let in your cabin?"

Scotty had grown up a lot. He was the same in some ways, and different in others. Now came the test. How could he answer his agitated father over the first meal at home. Doris tried to intervene in her usual way.

"Stan, do we have to talk about these things on Scotty's first night home?"

Scotty stepped in.

"Do you see this band-aid?"

Doris responded.

"I've been meaning to ask you about that, Scotty. Did you scratch your nose on something, like a tree? It doesn't look too serious."

"No. I stood up for our Jewish people to anti-Semite Ralph Messer, and got punched in the nose by him for it when I quoted the New Testament to him."

She put her hand to her mouth.

"Oh my."

"Dad, Mom, I've grown up in the last two months. I'm still your loving son, but I'm not the same. And Dad, with all due loving respect to you as my father, I'm not going to accept your fits of rage like I did before. I won't tolerate them. I'll walk out. Moses tells me not to accept them. David tells me not to accept them. Isaiah tells me not to accept them. And for what it's worth, *Jesus* does too."

There was a pregnant pause. Then Stan exploded.

"Who in the hell do you think you are?"

Scotty came close enough for his bandaged nose to touch Stan's and spoke softly but clearly.

"I'm your son, who is supposed to be a man since my bar mitzvah. But somehow, I never feel like one around you."

He pivoted around and walked upstairs. When he neared the top, Stan screamed out, "You come back here!"

Doris switched to just her index finger over her mouth.

"Shh-let him be, Stanley. Let him be. I just wish he would be able to sit here and eat his favorite meal. I cooked it especially for him."

Scotty remained in his room through dinner. He lay on his bed and thought about that other world—the Camp Chalutzim world—the morning Shacharit service, the sweaty Israeli dance with Bunny, the Israeli folk songs, the erev Shabbat meals on white tablecloths with the candles, grape juice, braided challah bread, and prayer—and of all things, Brandon Marks' New Testament, and Jesus. *Jesus.* What did he think of Jesus? A teacher once told Scotty he was just another of many Joshuas, Ye-ho-shuas in Hebrew. Brandon Marks knew that wasn't right. Scotty knew that wasn't right. He would go to a bookstore that week and get *that book.* He would figure out where to hide it beyond his parents' reach. But he'd figure that out another day. This night he would just figure out how to sneak down to the kitchen to grab some cookies he could eat in his room.

At that exact moment, there was a soft knock on his door. He hesitated, but knew he had to respond. He went over and slowly opened it. There was his mother with a tray on which sat the veal cutlet meal, complete with dessert. He let her in. She placed the tray on his desk. Then she turned and hugged him tightly.

"I thought you'd want your favorite meal."

"Thanks, Mom."

"I know you're changing. You're growing up. You were almost the last one in your class to lose your baby fat. Now you're almost ready to shave."

Then, as if she was anticipating his every concern, she continued.

"I'm so proud of the man you're becoming. You can have whatever book you want in the house. I'll talk to your father. He loves you very much, but he needs to trust you like I do. I know you'll end up choosing the right things."

Scotty had determined not to cry. He hadn't cried that whole summer at camp, much as he came close at times. And now, his bruised nose was the only part of his face that he wanted to have to explain to either of them. But Doris's words released the deluge. He began to weep in heaves, and she joined him. They stood there hugging and crying for at least the next five minutes.

Scotty knew he would go to sleep quickly that night, between the long day that started with boarding the bus home and the long cry with his mother. He also knew that sooner or later his mother would settle his father down. So, he made a conscious choice to put any concern over his dad's latest outburst out of his mind. He quickly undressed and then slipped between clean sheets on his thick heavenly mattress—quite the opposite of pancake-thin. As he laid his head down on his soft pillow, he felt a presence—*that* presence. And unlike before summer camp in the same bedroom, he moved his lips silently as he prayed to the God he knew was listening.

"Thank You for this summer, and for all You've taught me. I'm not the same. This next school year won't be the same. Nothing will be the same. I'm a little late, but I think I'm growing up."

Michael Robert Wolf lives in Cincinnati, Ohio with his wife Rachel, an artist who has authored several fine art books. *Late Bloom Summer* is Wolf's fourth novel. His third novel, *The Other; The Linotype Legacy*, placed in the 2019 American Bookfest Awards.